SPECIAL MESSAGE TO READERS

THE ULVERSCROFT FOUNDATION
(registered UK charity number 264873)

was established in 1972 to provide funds for research, diagnosis and treatment of eye diseases. Examples of major projects funded by the Ulverscroft Foundation are:-

- The Children's Eye Unit at Moorfields Eye Hospital, London
- The Ulverscroft Children's Eye Unit at Great Ormond Street Hospital for Sick Children
- Funding research into eye diseases and treatment at the Department of Ophthalmology, University of Leicester
- The Ulverscroft Vision Research Group, Institute of Child Health
- Twin operating theatres at the Western Ophthalmic Hospital, London
- The Chair of Ophthalmology at the Royal Australian College of Ophthalmologists

You can help further the work of the Foundation by making a donation or leaving a legacy. Every contribution is gratefully received. If you would like to help support the Foundation or require further information, please contact:

THE ULVERSCROFT FOUNDATION
The Green, Bradgate Road, Anstey
Leicester LE7 7FU, England
Tel: (0116) 236 4325
website: www.foundation.ulverscroft.com

DEATH DIMENSION

When airline pilot Robert Varden's plane is wrecked in a thunderstorm, he goes to bail out. As he claws his way through the escape hatch, he is struck by lightning and his consciousness fades into oblivion. Miraculously, Varden cheats death, and awakes in hospital after doctors succeed in saving his life. But he emerges into an unfamiliar world that is on the brink of devastating war, and where his friends are mysteriously seventeen years older than he remembered them . . .

DENIS HUGHES

DEATH DIMENSION

Complete and Unabridged

LINFORD
Leicester

First published in Great Britain

First Linford Edition
published 2017

A catalogue record for this book is available
from the British Library.

ISBN 978–1–4448–3275–4

Published by
F. A. Thorpe (Publishing)
Anstey, Leicestershire

Set by Words & Graphics Ltd.
Anstey, Leicestershire
Printed and bound in Great Britain by
T. J. International Ltd., Padstow, Cornwall

This book is printed on acid-free paper

1

London to New York

'My dear girl,' said Varden, a little impatiently, 'you've got the whole aspect of it wrong from the very beginning. How on earth can anyone prevent a war? I ask you! The thing's got to come; and to my way of thinking, the sooner the better.' He raised his glass of Sauterne and watched the face of the girl across the table.

She wasn't a bad-looking girl, he reflected. Not a patch on Viki, of course, but then a man who spent his time flitting back and forth across the Atlantic had to fix himself up with amusement at both ends.

She was very small. Her hair was a sheath of burnished copper that moulded to her skull. Varden liked the dusting of tiny brown freckles on her throat, but was never sure of the grave intelligence that so frequently peeped from the depths of her greeny-coloured eyes.

She was fiddling with a little piece of bread now, crumbling it between her fingers, rolling scraps of it to pellets on the snow-white table linen. Long brown lashes covered her eyes as she stared down at the wine glass before her.

'I don't think I've got it wrong,' she said. 'It's you, Bob, who is seeing things in the wrong perspective. You're the one who wants to blast civilisation to pieces.' Her eyes were suddenly fierce, as if she resented his most natural instinct. And yet it was what a lot of other people — normal, sober people — thought. The world was ripe for explosion. Even a man like Varden, just a flying man, a pilot on a freight run from England to the U.S.A., could feel like that — and argue about it with a redhead in a London night club.

'Listen,' he said, very gravely. 'It's either they who start it or our side. And if we aren't damn quick it'll be them.'

Her eyes were hooded again, avoiding the swift impatience of his stare. 'You're a fool!' she said quietly. For a redhead, she kept her temper well. She had one, but Varden had never tasted its whiplash as yet. Had he done so, he might have been more careful in his attack on her principles.

He glanced round at the crowded tables, the tiny dancing space where a herd of cattle milled in their paltry amusement to the tinny clamour of a band. It wouldn't last. There would come a moment when all this would dissolve in a great orange flash, he told himself.

'You're wrong,' he said more gently. 'I wish I could make you see it, Rhonna, because if I fail you'll get a nasty shock.'

She raised her head, looking him squarely in the eyes. 'I doubt it,' she said very softly. 'My father will stop it —' She broke off. 'Stop it dead before it really begins. He can, you know — if he's given time.'

Varden raised his glass in a mocking toast. 'Here's to luck,' he said. There was a cynical edge to his voice. To Varden there seemed only one way out of the stalemate mess the world was in. Like many others he counselled what all men feared in their hearts. Ignorance, perhaps. Or plain bloody-mindedness.

'I don't want to end civilisation,' he said. 'I merely want to ensure that it goes on in the way I've grown used to. That can only happen if we make our play first.' He reached out across the table, covering her fingers with his hand. She did not resist, just looked at him, wondering; trying to make up her mind, as it were.

'Once you start it you'll never stop it,' she said.

He shrugged. 'We'll finish 'em off too quickly for that.'

The red-headed girl gave a dry laugh. There was no trace of humour in it. Varden wished he'd never asked her out for the evening. This was too much of a strain. He thought of Viki in New York, and decided he liked her better. There were no complexes with that piece of womanhood! She was built for one thing, and one thing only. And she knew it, which was more to the point.

'All right,' he said wearily. 'Forget it, will you? No hydrogen bombs, no atomics, no death. Just you and I for a while, huh?'

She didn't smile. 'I haven't finished yet,' she said with deadly calm. 'You're not the sort of man I imagined when we met. There's a lot that's nice about you, Bob; but an awful lot more that's rotten.' She met his gaze frankly. 'And now will you take me home, please?'

Something hot and angry stung in Varden's brain, a branding iron going deep and being twisted. Small white spots appeared at the sides of his nose, round his mouth. Red ones on his cheek bones, spots of colour. There was none in his eyes.

'Very well,' he said, turning his head. 'Waiter!'

In the taxi a sense of guilt made him say: 'If I tried to apologise —'

'It wouldn't be any use,' she finished abruptly. 'Thanks for everything, Bob, except this last. You're very conceited, and you think that people ought to give you credit for thinking of everything first. I don't mean I'm sorry I met you. I'm not. I've enjoyed the experience, but when you jeered at my father's ability to keep the world sane, you finished yourself.'

Varden felt something slipping from his grasp; something he had never even held with any firmness.

The taxi stopped. Rain fell in a steady drizzle on the glistening pavements. The girl stepped out and walked in through the entrance of a building, not looking back.

Varden stood and watched her disappear, tapping a cigarette on his thumbnail as his eyes followed her. The taxi was still waiting. He grinned at the driver. 'I'll walk,' he said.

As the red tail light drifted away and was lost in the drizzle, he scowled and turned his collar up. He'd been a fool; and even if he wanted to fill in a few spare hours with Rhonna in the future, she'd turn him down. All because they didn't see eye to eye about war. Walking stolidly, he made for his own hotel. War. It had to come, no matter what people like Rhonna's father thought they could do to prevent it. Scientists! It was they who made wars, in a way, not stopped them. Yet ... She'd sounded very sure of herself. In spite of his scepticism, he wondered. And then he remembered again how definite Merrick was in his views. He ought to know. If a man in big business in New York didn't read the signs rightly, no one else was likely to.

Varden shrugged his broad shoulders resignedly. If there was going to be a war, let them get it started as soon as possible;

and let it be the right side who began it.

He went to bed in a restless frame of mind, thinking by turn of Rhonna Blake; Merrick, big and blustery; Viki, all woman. Maybe tomorrow night he'd be in better company. The girl with red hair and freckles was too intense.

★ ★ ★

Sitting up there in the cockpit of the two-hundred-ton jet-engined freighter, Varden raised his hand to the man on the ground. A green light winked from Flying Control. Stretching out in front was the runway, long and clean and black in the morning sun. He gunned the engines and the great plane rolled slowly round for a take-off. La Guardia Field in six hours flat ... that was the schedule. He glanced across at his co-pilot and grinned. 'Here we go,' he said. Peterson nodded and talked to the radio as Varden opened up and fired the take-off assisting rockets. Their added roar filled the cabin. There were no other people on board apart from Varden and Peterson; this was a freight run, pure and simple. And, like a thousand others before it, it was swift and uneventful; a smooth stratospheric flight in the year 2017. Six hours from take-off, Varden brought the monster plane down to a perfect landing on La Guardia Field, New York. Routine.

★ ★ ★

Merrick was a big man in every way — in his size, his manner and his influence. 'How's life in England?' he inquired. 'Do you still jog around with the Blake girl? Or are you faithful to Viki?'

Varden scowled and examined his glass of Scotch. 'I see her sometimes,' he answered evasively. 'She's a bit of a bore, and I get rather tired of being told that her father can stop a war from ever starting. That's the part that infuriates me.'

Merrick laughed. 'No one can stop it!' he said.

'Hmm ... I was wondering what men like Rhonna's father could do to prevent it.'

'Nothing! An old fool's pipe dream, that's all it is.'

Varden grinned crookedly. 'That's more

or less what I told her myself,' he said. 'She didn't like me for it.'

Merrick leant forward earnestly. 'You didn't by any chance discover what lines he's working on, did you?'

Varden shook his head. ''Fraid not.'

'I just wondered, that was all. No importance, but it might make a difference. Never can tell.' His speech became staccato.

Varden eyed him with sudden shrewdness. He really thought Merrick would be pleased if someone did start a war right now. It was a thought that caused him vague misgivings. Merrick wasn't that kind of man, he told himself. Then he forgot about it as Viki joined them.

Viki Rochelle was a honey-blonde with a flair for accentuating her physical charms. The ones that were not actually visible were so subtly suggested that a blind man would have known all about them. When she said 'Hello,' her voice was a pure caress. Not so pure, perhaps, but a verbal caress for all that.

★　★　★

The lights in Viki's luxury flat were fully in keeping with the sentiments and objects of the tenant herself. Varden looked about appreciatively as he lounged back in a deep-seated chesterfield with a highball in one hand and a cigarette in the other. Viki was changing out of evening dress. Varden waited, eyes half-closed, in the softly lighted room, thinking and dreaming as he had done on more than one occasion in this flat before.

When the door opened he turned his head. She stood there for a moment, watching him, smiling with that hungry mouth of hers in a way that made him catch his breath. When he set his glass down, his hand was not quite steady.

She moved slowly across to a radio cabinet while he fixed her a drink. The dim light gleamed whitely on her skin through the black lace wrapper she wore.

'Make it a strong one,' she told him huskily. The radio came on with a *plonk* and quietened as she tuned it in. Then the announcer's nasal intonation came across the air:

'Station XX4 with the latest news, folks.

We are glad to be able to make this announcement. Complete agreement has been reached between the two major factions of the civilised world, and there is now no possible likelihood of war breaking out.' The announcer paused for breath; paper crackled as he turned his notes. 'The executives and administrators of these two great blocs have been meeting in secret session, the result of which has just been published. Full details will follow as soon as this station gets a later report — but the main thing, folks, is that war has been averted! Nothing could be better news than that, and we are sure our listeners will join us in giving those boys a great big hand!' Again a pause for breath. 'And now —'

Viki turned the set off with a vicious twist of her fingers. 'Fools!' she muttered.

Varden, who was moving towards her with a glass in his hand, gave her a startled look. Her face was whiter than before, the full red mouth drawn tight in a way that was almost evil. For an instant the languorous eyes were slitted. Then she was in full control once more; but not before Varden was left with a distinctly uncomfortable sensation of having seen right inside her soul.

'Here's to luck,' he said, handing her the glass. 'No war, eh? That's a pretty important thing, honey.'

She shrugged elegantly, smiling again and standing very close in front of him. He looked down at the sheer seductiveness of her, forgetting what he'd glimpsed but a moment before.

'There will be a war, for all they decide,' she whispered.

'Come on over and sit down,' he said. His arm went round her slender, sinuous waist. She leaned back against it, teasing him.

'Don't you want a war?' she murmured. 'You'd enjoy it, wouldn't you? Think of the opportunities!'

He led her towards the divan. 'If a war broke out I'd see very little of you,' he whispered. 'That would hurt.'

Her eyes flashed. 'You'd have your Rhonna in England,' she reminded him wickedly.

Varden didn't answer. He wasn't going to get out of his depth with this girl as well.

Then he remembered that her solicitude for him didn't quite add up with that queer expression he'd caught on her face when the news came that peace was ensured. He might have tried to sort it out in his mind had not Viki herself turned his thoughts into other channels by an act as old as time.

2

Single Bed

The insistent voices on the radio stilled as the freight plane winged on its way. Peterson was listening intently, listening to the disembodied tones of the Met Office stating sober facts. He was worried by what he heard. Violent electric storms were building up in a line along the western seaboard of Europe, deepening in a cold front and moving fast. Varden stared ahead through the perspex, noting the black wall of cloud in front. It stretched north and south without a break. Peterson spoke to him, telling him the latest report. Varden tried to climb above the front, but the cumulo-nimbus towered far into the sky, its inner bowels riven by lightning and stirred by wind.

'She won't clear it, Pete,' he said. 'And we haven't the fuel to turn back now.'

They flew north and south, seeking a

break in the storm front. There was none. And in the meantime the front was forcing him further and further back across the Atlantic.

'Only chance is to try flying through it,' he said tersely. Peterson said nothing. They'd probably tear the wings off.

Varden put the nose down, built up speed to the limit, and streaked in, knowing that if he failed he'd be lucky to come out alive.

Darkness closed in on the plane, seeming to shut it away from the world of light. He felt a sickening jolt and was flying blind, the two hundred tons that carried him being tossed around in a way that was frightening. Lightning crackled and flashed all round them. The radio went dead. Varden could feel the concussion of thunder above the roaring whine of the jets. Peterson said something to him but the words were lost. Even in the sealed cabin it was icy cold; frozen rain slashed at the fuselage.

Giant hands seemed to catch and grip the aircraft, turning it over and over as if it were a toy. Varden was thrown against his straps, hurting his shoulder. To his horror, the plane would no longer answer the controls. Something had gone. He stared round wildly, but there was only the turbulent heart of the storm outside; and, thousands of feet below, the wind-lashed sea.

The freighter was losing height now, being hurled downwards as swiftly as the eddies had earned it aloft. They'd have to get out of the ship or go down to the sea-bed with it. Varden sweated and knew what fear was like. By a rough reckoning, the aircraft was a hundred miles west of Ireland.

He left the ship to do what it liked; there was nothing he could do now. It was out of control and diving fast. 'Come on!' he gasped to Peterson. 'Jump!'

They fought their way back and fitted 'chutes. Lightning played weirdly on the fuselage as they moved. Varden's hands were shaking. *You're yellow!* he muttered to himself. *Yellow!* He didn't like the thought. Losing sight of his companion, he groped for the escape hatch. It was then that the lightning struck.

One instant be was clawing through the hatch, praying wildly; the next he was bathed in a vivid blue blast of dancing light.

The crackle of it battered his brain to pulp. He sagged where he was, then was hurled across the sloping floor. From somewhere forward came a deafening crash. The fuselage seemed to burst in a bloom of flame, disintegrating, spilling its cargo; then the pieces fell, scattering like broken eggshell.

Peterson was dead when his body fell, but the slip-line of Varden's 'chute caught an angle of sundered metal and opened of its own accord. As his limp body drifted down in the wake of the wreckage, he seemed to see through the darkness of insensibility a second figure alongside his own, a figure that grinned with evil humour and mouthed at him cruelly — a figure that was identical to Robert Varden.

* * *

Varden was picked up unconscious by the Galway trawler *Rosy Sky*. He was transferred shortly afterwards to a naval corvette, and eventually rushed to a hospital in southern England — a big white concrete building with firm, ungiving beds, rubber-wheeled trolleys and rustling nurses.

They put him in a private ward with a single bed, a red screen, a wooden chair and a table. On the chair they put a black-haired Irish nurse with a turned-up nose and a temperature chart belonging to the patient.

Varden knew nothing about it. He might have been dead for all the interest he showed, but he was vaguely aware of not having enough room in the bed. Once or twice he tried to open his eyes to tell the other man to get out and leave him alone. The Irish nurse might have helped him if she'd known about it, but they'd only given him a single bed.

He came round, came back to life, in the middle of the night. He was conscious of numbness, then pain.

The Irish nurse sent for Doctor Shoreham, the finest eye specialist in the country. He came and bent over Varden, his keen face anxious and critical.

Varden opened his eyes, blank and bleak and dead-looking as the doctor studied them. They were like a pair of pebbles among the swathes of bandage round his burned jaw and cheekbones.

Shoreham looked at the nurse, nodding.

Varden could hear someone moving close to him, could smell them and sense them, but he couldn't see them. He thought he could see the other man who was taking up so much of the bed; but when he tried to speak and complain about it he could only gasp, and the gasp sent scalding pain through his throat where fire had eaten it. Before they could give him any dope he passed out again, sinking into darkness even blacker than the pit of his sightless eyes.

During the days that followed he came round several more times, living yet not alive, swimming in a misty world of pain through which he was dimly aware — when agony let up for brief lucid periods — that he was blind. The cold iron of bitter defeat entered his soul and he no longer wanted to live. What good was a man without sight? He asked the black-haired nurse once, but she couldn't tell him. He didn't know her hair was black. He asked the man who shared his bed, who tossed and turned so restlessly and wouldn't let him have any peace. But the man couldn't answer his question either. He was blind, too. He called the Irish nurse Viki, but her name was Kathleen.

They told him at last, told him when the pain was less and the spasms of bitterness longer.

'There's just a chance that we'll be able to get your sight back,' they said. He listened and wondered what the faces of these men were like.

'You can try,' he told them. 'But I'd appreciate it just as much if you gave me another bed, a bigger one. This other man wants all the room.'

They looked at each other helplessly. 'He's complained of that before,' said Kathleen. 'It doesn't make sense.'

The other man told Varden to complain more often, but there was a mocking note in his voice as if it wouldn't make any difference. '*You've got me for keeps,*' he added vindictively.

'Shut up!' snarled Varden. He called the other man a name that made Kathleen blush and the doctors frown. Then they went away and left him alone with his companion.

'*You see?*' said the man with a chuckle. '*It's rather funny, isn't it?*'

'I can't see!' snapped Varden. 'Who the

hell are you anyway?'

'*Robert Varden,*' came the answer.

Varden thought about it for a spell. 'You can't be,' he said. 'I'm Varden.'

'*That makes two of us, doesn't it?*'

'Go to the devil!' shouted Varden.

'*We'll both go, shall we?*' answered Varden derisively. '*Don't you have any girlfriends to visit you?*'

'Not while you're around!'

Varden sighed wearily. '*Too bad,*' he mused. '*I couldn't see them, but I might hold their hands. What about Viki, now? She was pretty good. Or that redhead we knew.*'

Varden was very still and quiet. The other Varden pinched his leg playfully, making him shout. Kathleen was startled, but he told her to be quiet and not fuss.

'*What's she look like?*' asked the other man in a whisper.

'I don't know, damn you!' he grated. 'I can't see her any more plainly than you can!'

'*She sounded pretty good to me.*'

'What does it matter what she looks like?'

'*Ah, you never know, my friend. Still, I suppose you are right in a way. We're*'

21

handicapped, aren't we?'

'I wish I could kill you!' muttered Varden.

'*You'd have one hell of a job, brother!*' came the curt reply.

'I'd still like to kill you!'

Kathleen was relieved when her tour of duty came to an end. She complained to the Sister about Varden's abusive language and threats. The Sister arranged a transfer for her.

For a while there was peace.

A week went by, and then Rhonna came to see him. She saw the specialist beforehand.

'We want to operate and give him a chance of sight,' he told her patiently. 'But he must help himself, you understand? At the moment he doesn't seem to care what happens, and he has some complex or other that worries us considerably. Perhaps if you talked to him for a while it might help.'

She walked rather stiffly when a nurse led her down the long white corridors to Varden's room. There was darkness inside and another nurse sitting in the shadows beyond a reading lamp with a green shade. Rhonna could barely see Varden on the bed.

She moved slowly and almost reluctantly towards him. His head was rocking monotonously from side to side as she looked down at him. She couldn't dislike him now. Only sympathy and hurt rose in her heart, swamping put those earlier emotions.

'Hello,' she said softly. 'It's me, Bob; Rhonna. I — I thought you'd like to talk to someone.'

His head became still, frozen by the words. Then the meaning of them sank into his mind.

'Rhonna,' he muttered. 'What the devil do you want?' He gave a cracked laugh. 'I suppose,' he added, 'you've come to gloat over me now! Well, they stopped the war without your help or your father's, didn't they?' His voice was harsh and bitter, full of calculating desire to hurt and harm this girl who had been his friend. He was hurting her because if he didn't, she would hurt herself. He wasn't any use to a woman now.

Rhonna's mouth tightened. 'I'm sorry,' she murmured. 'No, Bob, I didn't come to gloat. I just came to say I was sorry about what happened to you.'

The other man prodded Varden in the ribs. '*You're a fool to speak to her that way,*' he said. '*Make her stick around.*'

'Shut up!' shouted Varden wildly. 'For God's sake, get out of my *bed,* blast you!'

Rhonna swallowed, glancing hastily at the nurse in the corner. The nurse shook her head slightly, saying nothing. Rhonna cleared her throat.

'I'll go now,' she said, struggling to keep her voice steady. He mustn't know what she was feeling about him. There was a lump in her throat as she saw the ghastly grin that twisted his mouth when he gazed unseeingly at where she was standing.

'*Don't send her away,*' said the other man plaintively. '*You spoil my fun, you do.*'

'Listen,' said Varden in a dangerous tone. 'If you utter one more word I'll strangle you!'

Rhonna was crying softly, unable to stop herself, but he didn't know and she made no sound. She didn't dare to speak again for fear of letting him know the truth. When she stood outside the door in the cool, lofty passage and grabbed at what was left of her thin self-control, she could still hear the gall of his words. She wondered almost savagely if he would have spoken like that to Viki.

★   ★   ★

The eyes of the surgeons met across Varden's body. Heads were nodded silently, gestures made and answered. In the stillness of the operating theatre there was only the sound of breathing and the tiny click of surgical instruments. The white muslin masks bent and ducked as they worked, rubber-gloved hands busy.

At last it was over. The chief surgeon straightened up.

'All right,' he said quietly, his voice muffled slightly by the mask he wore. 'Take him away now. Complete darkness, absolute silence, please. I'll talk with the ward Sister myself.'

Varden came out of the anaesthetic to find himself back in the same single bed with the same man sharing it. The other man was snoring. Varden reached out a hand and felt him all over to make sure he was real. There was a lot he didn't understand, but one thing he did comprehend was that in some weird way this other man could talk to him so that no one else could hear. His bedfellow was, in fact, solid without being visible to outsiders. It came as something of a shock when he thought about it, but his head was aching too badly to think for long.

As soon as he tried to go back to the world of unconsciousness, however, the other man woke.

'*Have they finished with us?*' he inquired.

Varden said, 'Yes. Later on they'll take off the bandages and we might be able to see.'

'*Thank the Lord for that!*' was the fervent reply.

Varden said: 'Is your name really Varden?'

'*Of course it is!*' The man sounded indignant. '*Robert Varden,*' he said.

Varden scowled, but it hurt his face, so he stopped. 'Listen, Varden,' he whispered, hoping there was no one to hear, 'I'm going to make a pact with you. If you don't speak while I'm talking to other people, I promise not to complain about your behaviour in bed. Is it a deal?'

Varden laughed cynically. It was not a pleasant sound. '*I get you all mixed up, don't I?'* he sneered. *'It was me that sent the Blake girl off.'* He paused, considering. *'That was a pity, in a way. I think I'd have liked her. I always did go for redheads.'*

Varden shuddered uncontrollably. He felt as if he was going mad. And the man actually had the nerve to call himself 'Varden'. But how did he know Rhonna was a redhead, anyway? He turned over slowly, forcing a few more inches of room in the bed. The other Varden kicked him, and groaned when the sudden exertion brought pain to his body.

'For heaven's sake!' muttered Varden. 'Keep still, can't you?'

Varden was still for a time. Then he said, *'You just wait till we're out of here! Do you think I like this any more than you do?'*

'I don't care what you like!' he snapped. *'You will!'*

Days passed interminably. It seemed an age before they took off his bandages and gradually let the light reach his eyes.

At first it was too incredible to believe, but he could see again! After the first momentary wonder had passed, he looked carefully at the bed on which he was lying.

A bandaged face grinned back at him. The doctors watched him curiously, puzzled and worried when he choked back a sob in his throat and covered his eyes with his hands. Presently they went away and left him to get used to the idea of being able to see again.

'*You ought to be glad,*' said the man who shared his bed. '*You ought to be very glad, Bob. Think of the fun we can have!*'

Varden ground his teeth till pain wracked his face. The eyes were the same as his own, red-rimmed from the after-effects of the operation. He stared at them hard, trying to build up an explanation. But the rest of the face was heavily covered in bandages, just as his own was. And the light in the room was far too dim to he certain.

'I must be crazy,' he muttered.

'*If you are, then so am I, pal!*' The man sat up slowly at his side. '*Pity we can't see what we look like, isn't it?*'

'They took the mirror away,' said Varden.

'*Of course they did; they always do when a man's face is badly scarred. At first, I mean.*'

'Is your face burnt as well?'

A rasping laugh. *'What do you think? We couldn't be anything else after pranging that kite in the drink, could we?'*

Varden considered this. 'You mean the *Tempest*?' he said. 'She was a good crate till the lightning got her.'

'I know, I know! Wonder what happened to Peterson? He bought it, I suppose ... Too bad!'

'Nice guy, Pete.' Varden frowned. 'Here, what the hell are you talking about, anyway? Who are you?'

The other man worked his mouth in a grin, peering at Varden. *'I've told you several times already,'* he said. *'I'm Bob Varden, an airline flyer on the trans-Atlantic run. Don't you ever believe what you're told?'*

Varden covered his face. 'Oh, God!' he groaned. 'You're me, and I'm you!'

'You've got it right at last, brother!'

3

Complex Existence

The two Vardens sat on the edge of the bed, side by side, grim in their mutual antagonism. One was wearing a suit, the other was naked. A fat little doctor in a white coat and wearing rimless glasses was peering at the suited Varden earnestly.

'Now, I want to make if perfectly clear,' he was saying, 'that success may be only partial. You must understand that, and we feel it only fair to tell you.' He prodded the bed with a short, stumpy finger,

Varden stared back at him hard. He had a queer feeling that this little man might be the devil himself in another guise.

'Ask him what he means, Bob? Gloomy swine. All these medicos are the same.'

'What exactly do you mean, Doc?' asked Varden.

The rimless glasses flashed in the light. 'It may not last,' he told him flatly. 'I'm only telling you because you must come back here at the first signs of failing vision. We can probably save it then, but only if we catch it in time.'

'*Better not tell him we're seeing double!*' came the unbidden comment from Varden the Naked.

Varden squared his shoulders. 'Thanks,' he said. His voice was edged with the ghost of bitterness, but he put out a hand to take the doctor's in a brief, firm grip. 'Thanks, Doc,' he repeated. 'I imagine I'll get along all right.'

'*You bet we will!*' He was enthusiastic, now.

Varden said nothing, contenting himself with the pleasure of treading hard on the other man's bare foot. He had no wish to be detained on psychiatric grounds.

He was alone now, alone in a small white-walled room with a tall red screen and a single electric light in the ceiling. His naked self had wandered off with the doctor. *To have a look round*, he'd told Varden. It was a high, clean, bright room, and the window looked out across green grass and the ribbon of a distant road. Varden moved to the window, peering out, getting used to the notion that he could see again.

He avoided looking in the mirror only recently brought back to the room. He and his unholy twin had looked in it once, seeing the tracing of livid scar tissue and burn marks that even now had a tight sensation about them.

'So I may go blind again, eh?' he mused aloud, watching the distant road. 'With a face like mine, it might be better that way!'

Something moved along the road in the distance, something moving very fast. A silvery car of some kind; he couldn't recognise what it was. But it was going quickly. He looked up at the brilliant blue of the sky, finding that light didn't hurt as much as he'd thought it would. There was a plane of an odd design up there among the woolly clouds, he noticed. He thought about it very carefully for a minute, knowing that they'd never let him fly again. The well-remembered bitterness seeped round his soul. He set his jaw and turned away from the window to where his suitcase was already packed on the locker top.

He was snapping the locks when the

other Varden returned, grinning hideously. *'You ready to leave?'* he inquired.

'You're not coming, are you?' Varden loathed the idea.

The other rubbed his chin. *'I'll tag along for a while,'* he said. *'Just till I'm used to being on my own.'* He looked down at his body, rather thin from being in bed for so long. *'You know,'* he said thoughtfully, *'I do believe I'm getting solid. One of the nurses got out of my way in the corridor.'*

'If you go around without any clothes on, they'll lock you up!' snapped Varden impatiently. 'Good thing, too!' he added.

Varden nodded gloomily. *'Have to do something about it,'* he said.

Varden was picking up his case when there was a knock on the door. 'Yes?' His tone was curt.

The door opened to reveal a woman. She was smiling at him with the jaded smile of a wanton.

Varden whistled loudly and crudely. *'Bob!'* he exclaimed. *'Look, something from our murky past! Gone off a bit, hasn't she?'*

Varden frowned. There was something familiar about the face of this woman; he ought to know her. She was just over forty, he decided, a skilfully-enamelled face not quite hiding those few extra years that made her just too old. She stood there, leaning against the door jamb, smiling still. He went closer, staring into her eyes, trying to ignore the loose, pouchy skin beneath them, the hard-edged curve of her made-up lips, the tell-tale tinting of the whiskey-coloured hair. It had once been honey-blonde, he decided. He knew why she had been familiar now, knew who she was; but it didn't make a lot of sense. And her body didn't have that 'poured-in' grace about it either. Even corsetry couldn't hide those too-constricted bulges.

'Say something to her, you moron!'

He gulped. ''Lo, Viki,' he said, trying to smile. His voice sounded twisted, like his face. Nor did he fail to see the fleeting look of revulsion that flickered in her languorous eyes for an instant. She hated looking at him. He knew it instinctively, yet refused to let her see that he knew.

'Nice to see you, honey,' she murmured. Her voice was still the same husky cadence of bedroom promise. A shade less soft, perhaps, but playing the original tune. She swayed further into the room. Varden backed away, trying to orient his feelings. He had always imagined Viki would wear well. He supposed she had in a way, but he wouldn't have expected this. A lot of the softness was gone, to be replaced by a hard, intangible veneer that spoke of inner viciousness.

'I've got a car down below,' she said invitingly. 'I'll run you into town, take you out, Bob. That's what you need, and then later on ... ' She could still use her eyes.

'You're too kind,' he said, unable to keep the vague hint of a sneer from showing in his tone. How in hell had she come to alter so much? he asked himself.

She must have sensed that sneer. With a quick step she was standing close to him, trapping him against the wall before he could move away.

'You think I haven't cared, don't you, Bob? You think I've been enjoying myself all this time, waiting for you. What kind of woman do you think I am?' Her gaze was greedy and accusing at the same time.

'*Why don't you tell her?*' He was walking

round, scrutinising Viki from every angle, head on one side like a judge at a cattle show. Then he shook his head sadly. '*She's got something still, Bob, but it's not the same. Pity; with all that promise, too ...*'

Varden shot him a venomous glance that brought a frown to Viki's brow. *For the sake of peace,* he thought resignedly. 'All right, kid, let's go,' he said aloud. 'Of course I didn't think you'd forget me or leave me flat.' He picked up his suitcase, still thinking back through the past days when he'd lain in bed and prayed for death. That was before they'd let him see his face, or have his eyes uncovered in a lighted room.

The knuckles of his hand were white as he gripped his suitcase and moved to the door. The woman was close at his side; he could smell her heady perfume, and she was Viki, the supple-bodied girl of New York. Only she couldn't be Viki really. Viki had been twenty-five when he cradled her in his arms that last night before ... She could not possibly have aged and grown hard and brassy in that short space of time. He remembered every tiny detail about her. There'd been a small brown mole ... He turned his head and glanced at the woman, wondering if she was so like Viki that she had one there, too.

The other man grinned at him, reading his thoughts. *'I'll tell you later,'* he said. Varden ignored him.

'Where are we going?' he inquired.

'To have fun.' Again he caught a glimpse of that look of revulsion as their eyes met. They were in the long, white corridor by this time, walking not too fast, side by side, three abreast with Viki in the middle. A nurse came by. The naked man stepped politely aside. Varden was surprised at the way she was dressed. He'd never seen a nurse dressed like that. She wore a spotless white skullcap, a white shirt with a zipper down the front, and white linen slacks. In the next few minutes, he saw several more in the same type of outfit; it seemed to be general. They were smart, smiling at him politely as he walked with Viki.

In the wide entrance hall of the hospital he saw a calendar on the wall above the reception desk. Tall red figures in a multitude of black-edged squares. He was passing it now, eyes scanning it idly, then with more intentness as they focused.

'What day is it?' he said to Viki, or the woman who might be Viki if Viki was twenty years older.

'Friday,' she answered brightly.

'Friday, the twenty-fourth of August,' put in Varden grimly.

'The twenty-fourth of August,' added Viki, smiling. She shot him a sidelong glance. 'It was a Friday in August we first met. Remember, Bob?'

'At the Lavender Room on 42nd Street. She wasn't bad in those days, was she?' He scratched his ear, watching Varden over the top of Viki's head. Then he winked and postured with indecent disregard for convention.

But Varden barely noticed. He stared at the calendar, isolating the date with critical clarity. Friday, the twenty-fourth of August. But the calendar put the year at 2034. And the freight plane *Tempest* had crashed in 2017.

They were halfway through the door now, stepping out to a world of green grass and gravel and sunshine. Varden halted on the hospital steps and looked out across the lawn to where that distant ribbon of dazzling concrete stripped over the country.

Viki started down the steps ahead of him as a vehicle came round from the side of the block. She turned, her whiskey-coloured hair being stirred by the breeze, her eyes expectant as they rested on his face for a moment.

Varden glanced uneasily at the man beside him. 'What are you going to do?' he inquired in a whisper.

The man chuckled nastily. *'Get my bearings, brother,'* he answered. *'It's all a bit odd. It being 2034, I mean. Do you have any clues to that?'*

Varden shook his head, then started down the steps in the wake of Viki, this Viki who was seventeen years too old.

'Come on, Bob,' she called, with a hint of impatience. 'We're going places!'

'Yes, get a move on, man!' He kicked Varden so that he slipped and slithered down the rest of the steps on his back.

'That's in return for treading on my foot back inside!'

'You'll be sorry you were ever born,'

grated Varden.

'Why, darling, that's not a nice thing to say to a girl!' protested Viki lovingly.

The other Varden laughed. Varden decided he must watch his tongue more carefully. It was so difficult to remember that his conversations with his other half were one-sided to anyone listening.

He moved towards the car as a man in a one-piece uniform came and took his suitcase after opening the door. Varden studied the vehicle with genuine amazement. It was long and low and streamlined, with a fully-curved perspex hood over the whole of the seating space. But it only had two wheels, fore and aft. He could just see the bulging tyres beneath the low, flattened body.

The second Varden was wandering round it, sucking his teeth, examining details with inquisitive curiosity, frowning as he did so.

Viki entered the car with surprising elegance.

'I'll ride on the roof, Bob,' the other man said, winking. *'Wouldn't want to cramp your style, old man, but remember I'll be keeping an eye on you — so play fair in*

there.'

Varden mouthed something inaudible, then entered the car as Viki subsided against the cushions. Glancing upwards through the transparent roof, he saw the squatting form of his leering companion shadow. He shuddered and didn't look again. Later on, perhaps, he would be able to sort this out, he told himself; but just at the moment he was lost in a tangle of incredibility that was too much for his brain to grasp. It was 2034 instead of 2017, and there were two of him. And he was sitting next to a woman who had once raised the lust inside him but was now no more than a worn-out hag in the guise of a wanton.

The driver turned his head politely. 'The city, madam?' She nodded without speaking. Varden closed his eyes. When he opened them again, the two-wheeled vehicle was moving smoothly over the gravel. From somewhere in the car came the faint hum of engines. A rear-engined gyro-car, thought Varden. It was unbelievable; the whole thing was unbelievable. He almost began to believe that the faded woman at his side was Viki Rochelle after all. But surely it wasn't possible?

A long white dual carriageway opened out in front. Varden saw several other similar vehicles moving along it. He tried to estimate the speed of travel, putting it at something in the region of a hundred m.p.h. A small metal plate on the back of the driver's seat claimed the gyro-car as the property of the City Taxi Co. A hundred-plus taxi!

Presently they swept through a long tunnel, diving under a town. Varden saw the tall fingers of buildings rising above them as they dived. The tunnel was brightly lit.

When they came up he glanced back, seeing the cluster of the town fading in the distance. The car sped on as if on rails. He was conscious of Viki watching him curiously from the corner of her eye. The naked man on the roof was sitting cross-legged right above Varden's head, staring round with wondering eyes. He seemed to be just as intrigued by the scenery as the one inside.

'You find it strange?' murmured Viki.

Varden gave a start. 'I've been out of touch for quite a while,' he ventured.

She leant towards him, rather in the way

she used to when they'd been together in the past. Her perfume filled his nose for a moment. But the network of tiny, cobwebby lines round her eyes showed clearly through the make-up she wore.

'Seventeen years?' he muttered. 'This *is* 2034, isn't it?'

She nodded, snuggling closer against him as the muted hum of the engine wrapped them round. 'We don't alter much,' she said. 'There are things that time can't alter. You and me; the state of the world; and Merrick.'

'Merrick?' he echoed. 'I'd almost forgotten. How is he? How is he, Viki?' There was a fresh eagerness in his voice. But he remembered that neither of these people had been to see him in hospital. And that even Viki, despite her act, was at heart afraid and disgusted by his scars.

'You'll see him again before long,' she told him. 'He's in town, but busy.'

'Ah! He always was pretty busy. Still the big business man?'

'Bigger than ever! And when the war starts ... Boy, will he be big!'

Varden digested that item slowly. The

war? 'I thought they'd reached an agreement years ago,' he said. 'No more war.'

She gurgled with amusement somewhere down in her husky throat. 'You're such a child, Bob!' she said. 'This world was meant to suffer its wars to the day of extinction. You can't prevent it; no one can. Not even Blake and his cronies!'

Varden said nothing. The woman slipped an arm through his, leaning against him. The man on the roof tapped loudly and wagged a finger at Varden, grinning. Varden scowled and stared at the back of the driver's neck.

They were nearing the city now. Other highways led in, converging on the matted forest of pinnacle-like buildings. This was London, he thought incredulously. A different London to the one he'd known before. But older buildings stood cheek by jowl with modern ones; streets were wider but bore familiar names. There was a strangeness about the people, too. Their clothing was odd to his unaccustomed eyes. It was summer, and most of the women except the older ones wore shirts and slacks of some soft metallic cloth that shimmered as they walked. The men wore suits similar to his own — which, he noticed for the first time, was also of the same material.

Finally the car rolled to a stop. The man on the roof hopped down and stood watching the traffic for a moment while the driver got out and opened the door for Viki. They were outside a block of flats.

'Come on in,' said Viki silkily. She dismissed the car.

Varden hesitated. Then the naked horror that was part of himself said, *'Hurry, up, you fool! She's waiting for you!'*

She was waiting for him, tapping the toe of her shoe on the pavement, smiling with her made-up eyes. There was a smoky drift across them, the smoke of impatience or dislike perhaps.

For one blind moment Varden wanted to turn and run. He did turn, but was confronted by the other man. *'No you don't!'* he said firmly. *'We want to get anchored somewhere, and she's as good as anyone for a start!'*

Approaching Viki's apartment, Varden was surprised when the door opened of its own accord, automatically. The three of them entered, Viki in the lead, then the two men. Varden had a splitting headache and was worried. Viki worried him, and so did his constant companion, that separate entity of himself he was learning to loathe. It took a lot of getting used to, this new existence. And this living ahead of time, too. It had to be that, of course. He couldn't have been torpid for seventeen years in hospital. Something had happened to him, happened to his eyesight. Perhaps he wasn't where he was at all, but was only *seeing* this world of the future through his eyes. But was he seeing that other personality as well?

At the moment, the man was strolling round the big airy room and examining things with appreciative touches. Finally, he sat himself down in a chair at the other end of the room, watching Varden with cynical eyes, but quickly turning his attention to Viki as she moved about.

'Scotch, honey?' The voice of an older Viki, a more experienced Viki, but a less attractive one.

'Thanks,' he muttered, settling himself uncomfortably, one eye on his other self.

'She ought to modulate that walk of

hers,' observed the man. *'With all those bulges where there ought to be curves, she should be more careful.'*

Varden felt vaguely sick and apprehensive. He glanced at Viki as she came towards him, carrying a glass. Her hands were steady, but her eyes flickered with some inward fire, and her lips were bowed invitingly when she smiled.

'Play her along, brother! Nice and gentle, mind.' He made stroking movements with his hands, grinning suggestively.

'You damn well wait till I get you alone!' said Varden.

Viki purred. 'Darling, that'll be just wonderful, but we *are* alone.' She swayed against him.

Varden bit his tongue on the point of saying they weren't.

'Here's to us,' whispered the woman.

'To us,' he replied, working hard to manufacture a smile. It hurt his taut, scarred jaw. The Scotch was warming to his stomach when it reached that far.

'Look,' he said suddenly. 'I have a few things to do before we get together. First I want an hotel.'

She made a move at him. 'I believe you're shy of your little Viki,' she accused. 'But, okay, go ahead. There's the Carson next door. Go broody in there for a while. I'll still be waiting for you — here.'

'Now you're showing some initiative,' said the other with a nod of approval. ' *You and I have an arrangement to make.'*

Varden put his unfinished drink down, focusing his eyes to make sure they were steady.

'So long for now,' he said. He tried to slip through the door and leave Varden behind, but they went together in the end.

The Carson was luxurious, and the suite he rented comfortable. Both men strolled round it thoughtfully, finally coming to a halt and watching each other warily.

Varden was on the point of speaking when there was a buzzing noise from what he took to be a television cabinet. They both turned and stared at it as the screen glowed into life. Varden Two gave a whistle of admiration.

A girl's face with dental-cream-advert teeth was smiling at them. She was smiling in technicolour.

'Mr. Varden?' she inquired. 'Call for you.'

'*Which one of us does she mean?*'

'For me?' said Varden, frowning. 'What do I do?'

The Smile looked a little surprised. 'Why, you — you just take it, Mr. Varden; that's all.' She faded out, to be replaced an instant later by the fleshy features of Merrick. Varden felt a sense of disappointment at the change.

'Hello there,' he said, with an attempt at heartiness. Merrick talked loudly, telling him he was up in Scotland but was coming down south that night. In fact, he'd be in London in a couple of hours, and would call on Varden.

'*He must have got your address from Viki,*' said Varden Two in a sly aside. '*I'll bet they're pretty thick, those two.*'

'I'll pick you up then,' said Merrick, grinning more boyishly than his pouched face could stand.

'I'll be around.' He didn't want to watch Merrick any longer, not just now. He put a hand to the only switch visible on the cabinet. The screen went blind as he flicked it. Then he sat down again, gnawing his fingernails and scowling savagely at the smirking figure of his other self. 'Why don't you put some clothes on?' he demanded abruptly.

'But I'm not cold. If I wore clothes they'd show, and I'd still be invisible myself — except to you. That would start a riot when I walked around.'

'Damn you!' snapped Varden.

'And you, pal!' retorted Varden.

They sat and scowled at each other for several more minutes. Finally Varden rose to his feet and went towards the television affair.

'What are you up to now?'

'Just trying this gadget out. It's a video, I suppose. Quite an improvement on the telephone.'

'Uh-huh. Mind how you go.'

Varden flicked the switch and the Smile appeared.

'Can you connect me with a Miss Rochelle in the flat next door?' he inquired politely. The Smile asked if he had the lady's number. Varden supposed that an ancient telephone number in New York wouldn't do. He shook his head. The Smile said it didn't matter. The screen flickered again, and he found himself peering at the room where he had recently left a half-finished glass of Scotch.

Viki came prowling across the floor towards him, hipping it a little too much for grace.

'Lonely?' she inquired in a sultry tone.

Varden grinned crookedly. 'Not yet; just getting used to things, trying them out. Merrick called me a while ago. He's on his way to London.'

She nodded. 'He called me, too. Aren't you coming round? I'm still waiting.' A long jade holder was poised in her fingers, the smoke from a cigarette drifting up and tangling in her hair.

'Not yet,' he said. He was sorry he'd called her. And yet she was his only link with the past. She and Merrick. There wasn't anyone else, except ... except Rhonna Blake. But ... She wouldn't want him anyway, not now. The bitterness flooded him again, so that he turned off the video swiftly.

Varden Two rubbed his scarred chin reflectively. *'That dame,'* he said slowly, *'is up to no good, Bob.'*

'What do you mean?'

'*Look at it this way.'* He perched himself on the arm of a chair, wriggling his toes and staring at the carpet. *'She was never in love with us, not really. Why the devil should she cling like this to a couple of wrecks? I'm no beauty; nor are you! There's something behind it, Bob!'*

Varden considered him carefully. 'I think you're right,' he admitted. 'But just at the moment I'm in no state of mind to work it out.' He turned.

'Where are you off to now?'

'Out for a walk — and please, for the love of Pete, stay in here!'

Varden shrugged. *'Unsociable so-and-so,'* he grinned.

4

Mob Violence

The dusk of evening was settling over the city, being held at bay by the lights as they winked in a thousand windows. Varden mingled with the crowds, but could find no pleasure in them. He was a part of them, yet alien to them. Sometimes a stray pair of eyes would rest on him briefly, only to look away at what they saw. Loneliness cloaked him in a shroud.

He stopped and looked in a window. A street woman came and swayed alongside him, whispering. He turned his head and saw the red mouth and beckoning eyes. But her smile disappeared when she saw his face plainly. She moved on, leaving him alone with his loneliness. He'd find no comfort in her brand of pleasure. Even that hideously naked self who was waiting in the Carson for him would be company of a sort. But he walked on morosely, thinking.

Gyro-cars hummed softly along the streets, carrying parties pleasure-bent. The West End hadn't altered in that respect.

What was he going to do about that thing in his hotel room? Was he destined to support its presence for the rest of his life? The thought made him sweat. He couldn't understand how it had happened in the first place. Some strange and unknown force had split him into two separate and independent entities, and that was that. But was that other being only playful, or was it evil? He wished he knew the answer. And why, why was it 2034 instead of 2017? Life had been so simple in those days. Now it was a hell to be alive at all!

He entered a square where people were staring upwards at an enormous video screen on the face of a building. Varden realised it was a public newscast screen. The face of a man was up there, clear and well-defined.

'Lord Bungers, the Prime Minister,' whispered someone near him, telling a friend.

Varden peered hard at the man on the video screen. It was a strong face, with a heavy jaw and shrewd, dark eyes. A thin scalp of silver hair clung tightly to a high-domed skull.

Prime Minister of England, thought Varden. He liked what he saw, and there was a ring of stern authority in the words and phrases Lord Bungers was using, too.

' ... cannot tolerate for ever the abysmal degeneracy of the nations now ranged against us,' he was saying. 'It is not our wish, nor the wish of any sane nation, to crave war, but unless we can again reach agreement with our rivals we shall be forced to take up their challenge.

'Almost twenty years ago we did reach agreement. Differences were laid aside and nations were at peace in their own security. But now it is my solemn duty to issue the most grave and ominous warning it has been my lot to utter during this, my term of office. I have to tell you, the people of England, and the remainder of the civilised world as well, that we shall not hesitate to use our utmost endeavour in the event of catastrophic war being forced on this country.' The big jaw was thrust out de-fiantly, 'We shall not,' the Prime Minister continued, 'make war unless all other methods fail, but I impress on you all that there is a limit to abuse of the conference table.'

Varden glanced round at the faces of the people near him. The words of Lord Bungers rolled on in their grim and sonorous phrases. Nowhere did Varden see a smile or a smirk around him. Every man and woman in that silent gathering, grouped in their hundreds as they were, seemed absorbed by the unswerving strength of the man whose image they watched.

Only when the speech came to an end did the crowd seem to let go its breath. For a long second there was dead silence as the video screen went dark, then a tumultuous storm of cheering broke out and rolled and echoed back from the tall canyon walls of the street.

Varden stood amazed, being pushed and jostled by the milling crowd of which he was part. Then, somewhere not far from where he was, a man raised his voice, abusing the Prime Minister, calling the government a bunch of yellow wolves. 'They're afraid of war!' he screamed. 'Afraid to use all the devil's weapons they possess! Cowards!

Deceivers!' He was shaking his fist at the blank screen when Varden saw him last. Then the crowd closed in and shut off his view. He nearly went down himself in the melee. Above the shouting and swearing, a woman screamed on a high note of panic. Varden felt himself surging forward with the mob, unable to control his own movement. A fist caught him on the side of the face, but he barely felt the pain. In the dim distance he seemed to hear the wail of sirens. Mob violence in London!

The lights on the block fronts swirled as he turned this way and that on the eddies of the crowd. All round him, on every side, people were crying and yelling, cursing each other, the men at the top, the working man, the enemy and the State. A hundred separate fights were in progress between the factions, and this spot at any rate had already started its war.

It was then that the personal element entered and persuaded Varden to join in himself, briefly anyway. He was suddenly confronted by an individual with one black eye and blood running down his chin. The man didn't even bother to find out what allegiance he followed. His fist, a ball of iron, came sailing through the close summer night and caught Varden on the side of the jaw. Only just in time did he swing his head to avoid the full impact of the blow, but the balance of it made him see red. He felled the man and experienced his first taste of satisfaction since leaving hospital.

Another body catapulted against him, cannoning off his shoulder and staggering sideways. Instinctively, he reached out a hand and grabbed. A wriggling bunch of savage flesh turned and lashed at him wildly. Beyond the blows and the fear he saw a woman's features, drawn and scared and white. Then they suddenly exploded as another man forced himself forward, beating at the woman in a panicky attempt to break out of the crowd. Varden acted swiftly, without conscious thought. His free hand went out in a deadly punch as the man ducked and wove. But he still maintained his grasp on the struggling woman. He had to, because he dared not lose her now. She was just another link in this strange excursion through Time, a link with the Past and the Future as well. His fingers were steely hard as they bit down on Rhonna Blake's arm and dragged her towards him.

* * *

The park was quiet and dim, an oasis of peace. Varden sat on a bench with his eyes closed. The woman beside him was busy repairing her face.

They'd fought their way clear in the end, had run from the scene of the riot only just ahead of the police who dispersed it. As yet, no word had passed between them.

He heard a compact snap shut, then the bench creaked a little as she leant against it. Varden opened his eyes, grateful for the gloom. He was more grateful, perhaps, for the fact that his other self was not there to goad and taunt him. 'Good of you to get me out of that,' she said, taking the cigarette he offered.

'I recognised you.' He could feel her eyes on his face. It was too dark to see clearly, but he hoped she wouldn't shrink when he brought some light on the scene. 'How are you?'

'So-so,' she replied. Her voice was rounder, more adult; a pleasant voice with no harsh edges. 'I had an idea you were dead,' she added thoughtfully.

He flicked his lighter and cupped the flame in his hand. Rhonna turned to face him. The planes of her face were clean and firm, untouched by the mouldering of age. She must be thirty-seven or thereabouts, he thought.

'I want to see you properly, Bob,' she said.

A small pulse was beating sluggishly in the side of his neck. For a moment he sat there, stony and cold inside, with the warm summer breeze playing on his cheek.

'I'm not very pretty,' he muttered, un-cupping the flame of the lighter and letting its glow fall across his face. He could watch her as she stared at him, watch the gradual change of expression, the flicker of pity in her green-coloured eyes.

'I had to make sure,' she whispered. 'I'm sorry ... about your face, I mean. Does it ... hurt at all?'

A wild desire to laugh rose in his throat. She was sorry for him! Why did she have to say that? Why in the name of God couldn't she just have nodded and taken him for granted, shutting her eyes to the ghastly pattern of scars?

'Thanks,' he said hoarsely. 'But I don't need pity! I'm too conceited — remember? Too hard to care a hoot what people feel for me!' He thrust his face close to hers. 'You don't care what happened to me, Rhonna! You're too wrapped up in what will happen to the world if they start the war that's coming!'

She shrank back as if he'd struck her on the mouth. 'There'll be no war,' she whispered. 'They're too late now. We're almost ready. Just a few more days, and there can't be a war at all.' Her words were fierce. Then: 'I thought you might have changed, but you haven't.' With what was suspiciously like a sob she jumped up and fled among the shadows, leaving only the faintest trace of perfume behind.

*   *   *

It was late when he returned to the hotel. As he went in past the reception desk a bell-boy intercepted him.

'A Mr. Merrick called to see you, sir,' he said. 'He left a message to say, would you call him at Miss Rochelle's flat when you came in.'

Varden nodded in a surly fashion. He was thinking that up in his room that other being would be waiting for him, grinning sadistically. He went up in the lift.

'I've been thinking while you've been gone,' said Varden Two. *'And I've discovered that by thinking about you very, very hard, I can make myself partly solid. Maybe with practice I'll be as real to the outside world as you are. Remind me to try.'*

Varden scowled angrily. 'What are we going to do about us?' he asked. 'I've been thinking, too. You've got to keep out of my way, or you'll drive me crazy, then you wouldn't be too good yourself!' He poured himself a drink, glancing at the tilted bottle. It was half-empty. 'Have you been drinking this?' he demanded.

The other man nodded. *'Now and again.'*

'It drinks, but no one else can see it!' grumbled Varden. 'Are you going to be with me for always?'

He grinned. *'Heavens no! You're too dull, Bob! I'm calling on the lush Viki later on tonight, I think. Merrick was here earlier on, by the way. He's someone else after us for no good.'*

'I'm supposed to call him at Viki's place.'

'Go ahead. See what he wants.'

Varden crossed the floor to the video and flicked it on. A different Smile with long, dark hair and a small, tilted nose came to life on the screen. Varden was put through to Viki's flat without delay. She was curled up in the corner of a settee like a Persian cat, with Merrick bending over her confidentially. He straightened up at once, recognising Varden.

'Ah, there you are at last!' he blared. 'Thought you must be out on the tiles all night, Bob. Why not come on round for a drink?'

'Yes, do that, honey,' put in Viki's syrupy tones from the background.

Varden shook his head. 'I've earned my sleep tonight,' he said. 'Got involved in a riot in town.'

Merrick growled. 'A pack of fools!' he said. 'They don't know what they're talking about. They're much too yellow to risk a war! They'll just hang on and hang on till the other side starts it, then it'll be too late. We've got to start it first, I tell you!' His face, already florid, was redder than ever. Why did a man work himself up like that about a war? Varden wondered dispassionately.

'*That guy wants one badly,*' muttered Varden Two. *'He'd start it himself if he could. Personal gain, if you ask me.*'

Merrick said, 'Forget it, Bob. How are you fixed for a job these days? I could help, I think.'

Varden eyed him narrowly. 'See you in the morning,' he said. 'In the bar downstairs. If you have any ideas, I'll be glad to listen. So long.' He switched off the video before either Merrick or Viki could say any more. Then he turned and glared at his companion, now smoking a cigarette in evident enjoyment of the situation.

'Don't you ever sleep?' he demanded tersely.

The man who was Varden shook his head. '*When you sleep, I live,*' he said laconically. '*You've had enough for one day, brother.*

Go on and turn in; I shan't disturb you this time!'

Varden was genuinely tired. He said nothing more, but undressed. Varden Two tried his clothes on, found they fitted, and walked round with annoying solidity. Just as Varden shut his eyes and set to wooing sleep, the other man went quietly out, closing the door behind him.

5

No Peace for the Dead

Merrick didn't waste any time in coming to the point. His eyes were hot and angry when Varden entered the bar next morning.

'You're a damn fool to walk around as if you didn't have a care in the world!' he said, glancing round cautiously as he spoke. He kept his voice low, too.

Varden frowned. 'Why should I hide myself?' he demanded. 'I've come for a job from you, Merrick, and I mean to have it. I want to get out of this city and go a long way fast. Start all over again.'

'I'm not surprised.'

Varden gave another frown, peering curiously at Merrick. 'What's the matter with you this morning?' he asked. 'Aren't you satisfied with the threat of coming war?'

Merrick flushed darkly. 'You don't seem to have a conscience,' he grunted. 'But if that's the way you want it, all right. I've got a job for you, but whether you can do it now, I'm not so sure.'

'What's the job?'

Merrick ordered a drink for both of them before answering. Varden saw that there was no sign of Viki; she hadn't come down with Merrick, apparently. He thought about his own position and the problem of getting away from that other entity now in his room. If Merrick could fit him up with a job, he'd just leave and not go back at all.

Merrick eyed him calculatingly. 'Let's talk about war,' he said. 'The one that's coming,'

Varden shrugged. 'I thought it couldn't start,' he said. 'Scientists and things ... '

'Rubbish! It's going to start, and I'm going to start it!'

Varden sipped his drink. 'You are, eh? Where do I come in?' He decided that Merrick must have a very bad liver this morning. Almost as bad as his own!

Merrick leant towards him. 'I want to know what Blake and his pals think they can do to prevent a war,' he said earnestly. 'That's your job, Bob; though how you're going to do it now, I fail to see. However ... '

'Just a minute,' said Varden bleakly. 'Where do I find the Blake girl? She'll be my best line of attack.' He did not want to probe into Rhonna's affairs regarding war, but he did want to locate the girl again and try to apologise for being so rude last evening. Here was a way of doing it.

'Don't treat her like the other three, Bob. It wouldn't pay!'

'I'll treat her any way I like!' he snapped. 'Give me her address and let me get out of here. You're like a bear with a sore head.'

Merrick said nothing, but scribbled something in a black notebook and tore out the page. 'There you are,' he said. 'Keep in touch with me by video, but don't come to Viki's flat.'

Varden's jaw tightened. 'She's my woman, isn't she?' he demanded dangerously. 'Or has she changed her mind? Not that I want her, mind, but I'm curious.'

'Keep away,' Merrick told him. 'That's all!'

Varden sneered. He felt bitter today, more so than yesterday. 'In that case,' he said, 'you can chase Blake for his secrets on your own. I'm through with you!'

Merrick's eyes narrowed. 'You're hot,' he said. 'If you don't obey my orders, Bob, you'll be on trial inside a week!'

Varden felt a chill of fear creep down his spine. 'Why?'

Merrick gave a short laugh, more sure of himself now. 'You don't have to ask me that,' he said. 'Get going on the Blake girl, and don't try to pull any tricks or you'll suffer. I want full details of the old man's activities, and you're the person to do it. Now move!'

Varden left the bar in a puzzled, angry frame of mind. He did not understand Merrick's attitude. Last night on the video, the man had been affability itself. Now there was an underlying hint of blackmail in his approach. He wondered if the man could actually start a war of his own. It didn't seem possible — yet Merrick was a man who never said impossible things. And Varden himself was accepting this task because he wanted to contact Rhonna again, not because he wished to help Merrick by worming secrets from Rhonna's father.

He stumbled into the street and stood gazing at the busy scene. Once again he seemed to be on the brink of a world that was strange and alien to him, but now there was a shadow behind him, a shadow contained in what Merrick had said and hinted at. He wondered about it, but could reach no definite conclusion.

He was turning towards the Carson Hotel when a blue-uniformed patrolman approached slowly down the street. Suddenly the man paused in his stride, staring at Varden intently. Varden gave him look for look. His temper was frayed and he didn't care what happened now.

The patrolman, however, didn't stare for long. He broke into a run, straight for Varden. Varden watched him coming for a second or two before he realised the man was making for him. Then he remembered. Merrick's strange attitude. Something was very wrong, he thought wildly.

He started running himself, glancing over his shoulder to make sure. The patrolman was close on his heels, shouting now. People stepped into Varden's path, trying to bar his way. He crashed a man in the face with his outstretched hand, sending him spinning. He thought he heard the word

'Murderer!' but didn't believe it. A woman hurled a shopping satchel at his legs, but he jumped clear, then dived for the roadway, panic rising in his heart because he didn't understand and was frightened.

Next instant there was a rushing hum in his ears and a swiftly-moving gyro-car swept towards him, the white face of the driver showing with dreadful clarity behind the screen. A siren wailed and the brakes screamed. A woman shrieked. Varden saw it coming a second beforehand. He leapt, but no human movement could avoid the inevitable. He felt a frightful impact on his body, then was hurled yards along the roadway, to finish up a crumpled heap of flesh against the offside curb. He saw some dust and scraps of paper in the gutter under his nose, but lights jazzed and whirled in his brain and blotted them out.

The whole of his body was one mass of flaming agony, but he was not unconscious, which puzzled him. He lay where he was, hearing running feet and the agitated whispers of people all round him, people in the presence of a sudden tragedy. Someone bent over him. The white, startled face of the driver.

'He's dead!' the man breathed. 'It wasn't my fault!' Suddenly his face changed. 'It's *him*!' he cried.

The patrolman thrust him aside. 'Yes,' he said tersely. 'It's him all right! You've saved the courts a job, by the look of it.' He knelt beside Varden and fumbled. Varden kept his eyes on the man's face, trying to speak. He could not move a muscle. The patrolman was holding his wrist, hunting for a pulse. But Varden couldn't feel it now. There was no pain any more, nothing but a dreadful stillness. He could not even feel the beat of his own heart.

The patrolman shook his head. He was breathing heavily. He was saying something, but Varden could not hear now. Then a man with something white pushed his way through the crowd and unfolded a sheet. The folds of it blanked off Varden's vision. And the dreadful stillness inside him and all round him was worse. Not even his heart … God, he thought, he was dead! He was *dead*!

★ ★ ★

Varden sat up slowly, peering round. The place was cold and bare and it took time to register in his mind that he was inside the morgue. They'd taken his clothes away and left him a sheet, nothing more. A sheet that smelt faintly of death and had covered him on a cold steel slab.

He wondered what to do about it. It was an unpleasant shock to find oneself laid out tidily in a morgue. He got up and walked about, holding the sheet round him for warmth, then he remembered what had happened and stopped in midstride. He'd been killed in a street smash escaping from the police! But he didn't feel as if he'd been hit by anything. There wasn't a bruise on his body, nor a stiff joint. He sat down on a chair and pondered, wondering about it. He had been killed. He knew that, and yet he wasn't dead.

A door at the end of the room opened and a man came in, busy looking at a folder of papers, hurrying across the floor to a desk, not glancing in Varden's direction at all.

Varden coughed loudly. 'I say,' he said.

The man halted abruptly, seeing him for

the first time. Then the blood drained from his face and he screamed brokenly.

'Hey, wait a minute!' shouted Varden, bounding after him as he turned to flee. 'I want to talk to you!' He reached the man in a few strides, seizing him by the scruff of the neck.

'Now, look here,' he began savagely. But his victim went off in a faint, collapsing in a heap on the ground. Varden swore.

Fortunately, the door was closed, and apparently no one else had heard the outcry. He waited patiently. Presently the man came round, terrified again when he caught sight of Varden.

'You — you're dead!' he stammered.

'I'm not!'

'But — but you *must* be! You came in here with a broken neck and multiple fracture of the skull.'

'I don't even have a headache right now.' He thrust his scarred face close to the man's, terrorising him. 'Tell me this, little man,' he said grimly. 'Why were they chasing me?'

The man gulped violently. His eyes fled to the slab on which Varden had been lying.

'You — you're a murderer,' he whispered. 'You killed three women and one man last night. Every person in the country knows about you! You'll never get away with this!'

'I did *what*?' demanded Varden incredulously. Then he stopped, an awful thought flooding through his mind.

'You killed three women,' the man repeated. 'After the most savage assaults on record. The — the man tried to stop you in one of them, but you killed him too!' His teeth were chattering.

Varden let him go, feeling weak and sick himself. The man watched him apprehensively. Varden said, 'You're staying here, my friend. I want your clothes. Quickly!' His voice rose.

The man swallowed, but hurriedly undressed. Varden pulled the ill-fitting clothes on his own frame, then measured the distance carefully, and cracked the man on the side of the jaw with the force of a pile driver. He went down without a sound.

It was night outside, for which he was grateful. The first hint of understanding was coming to him now. His other self, that ghastly entity that had sprung from his own being, was evil, not just playful and mischievous as he'd thought before.

He left the morgue through a side door that opened in a narrow entrance shrouded in darkness.

'If that car didn't kill me, I can't be killed,' he said to himself. 'Is that good or bad? I'm damned if I know! But how did that other being manage to commit murder? He has no substance except to my eyes, and that can't be real!'

Before leaving the morgue he had found an old hat, which he kept pulled low on his face. No one gave him a second glance. The four-times murderer was dead, killed on the street. They weren't looking for him now, therefore they didn't see him. But he went cautiously for all that. And getting to his room in the hotel was likely to prove difficult.

He chose the fire escape at the back as being safest.

'Hello there!' he was greeted on entering via the window. *'I hear you've been having adventures.'* The words were said cynically, with a dry sense of humour that maddened Varden further.

He halted in front of the other man; standing over him, eyes blazing.

'You ...' he said between his teeth. 'What did you do, damn you?' He thrust out a hand and gripped the other by the throat.

Varden Two laughed. *'You can't do that,'* he protested. *'They can't kill me any more than they can you! Don't you realise that, Bob? We're immortal. We aren't living in 2034 any more than we're living in 2017. We're footloose in Time, if you can comprehend. I've been working it out.'*

Varden still retained his grip. There was too much cold anger inside him to let go yet. 'You killed four innocent people,' he grated. 'Three of them women. And what's more, I get the blame and get killed for it!'

His own eyes stared back at him, mockingly. *'It was fun,'* came the answer. *'It's enlightening to know you can kill and not be killed, Bob. Power over life and death! I called on Viki, too. She was glad to see you, Bob.'* He smiled. *'She still has her points, I might add, and when I'd finished I told her about the others that night. But I didn't kill her, even if she thought I meant to.'* He giggled wildly. *'Shook her a bit, I must say, because I made her believe it was true. I gave her all the authentic details, you know!'*

'You sadistic swine! And Merrick wanted me to work for him so that millions of people would die in a futile war, just to please his own vanity! If you were killable, I'd kill you myself!'

Varden Two laughed harshly, pushed his arm away and walked up and down the room for a spell.

Varden got a much-needed drink for himself. There was very little left in the bottle. 'How did you do it?' he said, at last. 'Make yourself solid, I mean. You aren't usually.'

'When you sleep, brother, I live. I've told you that before.' He lit a cigarette and inhaled deeply. *'You've got to remember that we only have one body between us.'*

Varden rubbed a hand across his eyes. 'Then I can't ever sleep again!' he muttered tiredly. 'Oh, God, why did that plane ever crash?'

The other man regarded him thoughtfully. *'What are you going to do now?'* he said presently.

78

'That's the last thing I'd tell you!'

'Please yourself!'

Varden walked across to the video cabinet, hesitated, then changed his mind. He couldn't show himself to the Smile now. He went out through the fire escape again, leaving the other man sitting comfortably in a chair, drinking.

In one of the many street booths he called up Viki's flat.

She was weary and frightened-looking when he saw her face. All the voluptuous seduction had gone from her eyes. 'What do you want?' she asked, startled at seeing him. 'I thought you'd been killed in a road accident. You deserve to be!'

Varden shook his head. 'Not me,' he said flatly. 'That was another part of me. Not me.'

Her eyes flashed fire for a moment. 'It was you who nearly slaughtered me last night!' she told him. 'What do you take me for? A fool?'

'Stop making me mad,' he said. 'I need your help badly. I'm coming round and coming up by the fire escape, understand? Don't try any tricks, Viki.'

'You can't come here!' she gasped. 'Not after ...'

'I only want your help,' he cut in. 'See you in a few minutes. Be waiting for me.'

Merrick was there as well when he arrived. Varden did not attempt to explain about the second entity; he knew it would be a hopeless task. They were wary of him, but put on a front of apparent friendliness that made him smile secretly.

'Have you been on to the Blake girl yet?' asked Merrick.

Varden shook his head. 'I was killed this morning just after leaving you,' he said thinly. 'I didn't have a chance.'

Merrick tried to chuckle. Viki went a little paler.

'If I was recognised, they'd get me again,' said Varden. 'I want Viki to treat my face with cosmetics and greasepaint and blot out these cursed scars enough to cover my identity. And I want fresh clothes. And my hair dyed another colour. Now get moving, please. I have a job to do.'

For a wonder, neither of them raised any objection. Viki went so far as to suggest that maybe Varden could do with a snatch of sleep while she was getting what he needed. But Varden only laughed. Sleep was the one thing he dared not indulge in.

While he was waiting he talked with Merrick, probing with all the cunning he could command in an effort to find out how the man intended to start the war.

'You don't need to know, Bob,' he was told. 'It's better that you don't. You do your part, and I'll do mine.'

Varden pretended disappointment. 'But how do I know I'm not risking my neck for nothing?' he protested. 'How do I know you can actually start this thing and get away with it?'

Merrick smiled knowingly. 'I can do it,' he insisted. 'At a few hours' notice I can plunge the world into war! But it will be *our* side that starts and does the most damage first. We'll bring 'em to their knees, Bob.' His eyes narrowed. 'And we'll make money from it.'

'That's all you really want from it, isn't it?'

Merrick tut-tutted indignantly. But although he denied the accusation stoutly, there was little conviction in his words.

Viki returned soon afterwards with

everything he needed. How she'd managed to get the stuff at that time of night, he didn't know, but apparently she had ways and means. She even had a suit of clothes that fitted him passably well.

When he looked in the mirror he could hardly recognise his own features, so skilfully had the woman made him up.

'You look almost handsome,' she said, with a trace of the old accent. But he noticed that she kept well out of his way when he moved towards her.

'Thanks, Viki,' he said. 'I'm going now, and I'm really grateful for what you've done. I shan't trouble you, but if that other man who looks like me does happen to come around, you'll know him by the fact that he looks like I did a while ago. Bear that in mind, and be careful.'

She nodded dumbly, afraid of him, yet trying to be fair.

Dawn was breaking when he left the block of flats, tired and sick at heart, but filled by a new determination. He could not even die; there were two of him; and he was living in a time dimension to which he did not belong. Those factors were enough to make any man worried, especially with the knowledge that he was wanted for multiple murders as well.

6

Varden Strikes

Confident that his disguised features would conceal his identity, Varden walked boldly through the half-light of breaking day. He was faced by a number of problems, to none of which did there seem to be any quick solution.

He was halfway up the fire escape when he became aware that the naked figure of his other self was sitting languidly on the metal steps outside the apartment window. Cursing under his breath, he came to a halt. Suppose he pitched the creature down the escape? Would it die?

'You can't go back in there, Bob,' said Varden Two, grinning. *'Someone else just moved in. Late arrival at the hotel, and they gave 'em our room because you're on the run. They know you aren't dead, by the way. The morgue broke the news.'*

Varden sat down thoughtfully. Now

what? He must get in touch with Rhonna, tell her what Merrick planned. But would she even see him, let alone listen to the word of a supposed killer?

He got up and glanced in through the room window. A large man was asleep in bed, his stomach rising and falling as he snored. It was true, then. And it meant that he must find somewhere else to hide up till he contacted Rhonna.

'What are you worrying about, brother?'

'Lots of things, damn you! They'll still be looking for me, I suppose.'

The other man chuckled. *'You're in quite a spot, aren't you? But listen, I'm on your side. As soon as I was more or less evicted from in there I thought: 'Poor old Bob, he must have somewhere to lie up for a while.' So I went and found a spot quite handy. Come on, I'll show you.'* He stood up and started down the fire escape ahead of Varden.

Varden felt a hot rush of anger coursing through his body. He placed his shoe flat in the middle of Varden Two's back, and thrust him out and down. For a moment, he thought he'd succeeded; then the man came floating back at him, a sneering laugh on his lips.

'Don't you ever learn?' he demanded. *'That's no way to act when I'm trying to help you. Come on, for Pete's sake!'*

Varden stared with loathing at the face that was his own, at the sinewy body that was his, and the cold, sadistic eyes that were his and yet not his. He knew he was beaten.

Varden Two led him down the fire escape and through an alley to a gloomy entrance that gave onto a storage yard. Varden Two was carrying a bottle of Scotch, a full one — or almost full. Inside the yard was a shed, partly cluttered with odds and ends.

'Cosy, isn't it?' He waved his free hand possessively. *'Have a drink, Bob. Make yourself at home; it's yours for as long as you like, with the compliments of the management!'*

Varden peered round uncertainly. The rubbish and litter ranged from an ancient bicycle to a pile of ragged clothes. He sat down wearily on a broken-backed chair and stared morosely at his companion.

'Well?' he grunted.

Varden Two opened the bottle of Scotch

and held it out with an inviting gesture. Varden took it and drank. The spirit stilled some of the confusion in his mind, but his weariness only increased. He sat leaning forward on the chair, head in his hands as he struggled to think clearly. Varden Two squatted on the floor, watching him with cynical amusement.

'*Tired?*' he inquired lightly.

'Shut up!' snarled Varden savagely. 'If I have to walk about for the rest of my life, I shan't sleep again!'

'*Not unless you can't help it, brother!*' There was a note of craftiness in the words that made Varden sit up sharply. He found it difficult to keep his eyes open now; his vision was blurring.

'You devil!' he got out. 'That whiskey ... '

'*Was doped, Bob. Sorry, but I have to get around in the flesh at times. Just take it easy and relax.*' He laughed '*I rifled a chemist's shop for that stuff, and I know it's good!*'

Varden struggled to rise to his feet, but lead weights were round his neck now. He saw only dimly, and the dimmer he saw the more helpless he felt. The other man was putting on clothes from the pile on the ground now. He grinned at Varden, then raised his hand in farewell as he made for the door of the shed.

'You'll murder again!' Varden croaked. 'You'll kill!'

Varden Two paused, looking back. *'I'm going to see Viki,'* he said. *'Strictly business, brother! Sleep well: you've drunk enough to keep you quiet till midday!'*

Varden tried to speak again, but instead he flopped on the chair and slid off it to the ground. Varden Two chuckled and covered him with an old coat. Then he was gone.

* * *

Sunlight seeped in through cracks in the wall and roof. Varden opened his eyes and sat up with a jerk, to sink back instantly as stabbing pain wracked his skull. He groaned, then remembered with the full force of horror what had happened. That other entity was loose again, had been solid flesh and blood during the whole of the time he slept in a stupor! He stood up painfully, shaking his head. But the other man would not be solid now, he realised. There was only one body between them, he remembered. God, what an abomination this was!

He moved cautiously to the door of the store shed and peered out anxiously. There was no one in sight, but he could hear voices nearby drifting through an open window in the block that formed one side of the yard.

It was then that he saw his other self coming towards him across the yard. Seeing Varden, the now-naked entity waved a hand in sarcastic greeting.

He opened the door and came in. *'News, Bob,'* he drawled.

Varden gripped him by the arm, blind hate surging inside him. 'Have you killed anyone?' he said between his teeth. 'Answer me that! Have you made me a murderer again?'

The other looked at him reproachfully. *'Take the weight off your feet,'* he sneered. *'Didn't I say I was out strictly on business when I left you? No, Bob; no murders, no fun and games at all. Even Viki wouldn't co-operate this time!'*

Varden relaxed a little, not knowing whether to believe him or not. He sat down on the broken-backed chair and studied the man with a sour gaze. 'Well?' he demanded. 'What have you been doing then?'

Varden Two took his time, lighting a cigarette from Varden's case with exaggerated care. At length, he said: *'It's a pity in a way that I played such havoc among the women the other night,'* he said. *'Viki was really difficult when I walked in on her. She gave a yelp and tried to call the police!'* He laughed. *'The police, of all things!'*

Varden said nothing. He was suddenly sorry for Viki. She meant nothing to him now, but he was sorry for her all the same. 'What happened?' he asked bitterly. 'Did you force her to play your games after all?'

Varden Two sighed. *'What a mind you have,'* he said, *'No, there'll be plenty of time for pleasure later on. I wanted to know about Merrick's plans, pal, and I think I've got the goods.'*

'Did she talk?' Varden was suddenly interested in spite of himself.

The other man nodded slowly. *'After a little gentle terrorising,'* he said with a smile, *'I did get enough to go on with.'* He paused. *'Are you interested, Bob?'*

'Of course I am! I'm supposed to be working for Merrick! He won't act till he knows what Blake has up his sleeve — if anything — which I can't really believe.'

'*He's pretty much afraid of what Blake can do,*' was the answer. '*More so than I thought in the first place. You'll have to go ahead with your part of it and find out for him — and for me!*'

Varden's eyes narrowed. 'Why for you?' he snapped.

'*I think a war might be fun, but Merrick is only out for gain, of course. And Viki tags along because she really belongs to him. We only come into the picture because we form a link with the Blake girl — and, via her, with the old man.*'

'What did you discover?'

'*Merrick is in a position to plant a guided projectile on London and New York. The world is in such a state right now that one bomb on any of our cities would be enough to start the war. By doing what he intends, Merrick will force our hand, and the government of this bloc will be pitchforked into hostilities. Now do you follow the reasoning? It's simple and direct,*'

91

and, by heaven, it'll work!'

Varden frowned. 'You mean our side will assume as a matter of course that the potential enemy did the bombing?'

'Exactly!'

Varden stood up and took a turn round the shed, the eyes of his companion following him reflectively. At last: 'I'd better get on to Blake, I suppose.'

Varden Two grinned. *'Don't try double-crossing Merrick,'* he advised.

Varden whirled around. 'Do you imagine I'll stand by and see this happen to the world?' he flared. 'I didn't use to give a hoot about a war being started, but I've had time to think since then! I'll do what I like, and you can't stop me!'

The other blew smoke towards the roof of the shed. *'No?'* he answered. *'All I have to do is knock you cold and just borrow the Body for a while.'*

Varden felt a chill foreboding at the words. 'Yes?'

'Yes. You wouldn't want anything dreadful to happen to that sweet little red-head, would you? I'm quite a master at it now, you know! Four killings to my credit.

92

Yours, I mean. But before I killed those women ...'

'You unspeakable monster!' Varden's voice was no more than a whisper, dragged from his throat by sheer hate. Before the other man could move Varden had seized the whiskey bottle and smashed it full in his grinning face. The bottle shattered, raw spirit running up his arm and broken glass tinkling on the floor. He stepped back, his hatred spent. He couldn't kill this thing that was part of himself. He knew it, but the force of his attack had been enough to kill any living man.

Varden Two sank to the floor. There was blood pouring down his face, dripping on the ground, spreading over his chest. He raised his head and stared at Varden with blazing eyes. But he said nothing. Varden dropped the broken neck of the bottle. His eyes were fixed on his enemy, staring incredulously.

Varden Two rolled slowly over on his side, to lie quite still. Then he gradually faded and became invisible to Varden.

'I can't have killed him!' he breathed, in a sudden surge of hope. 'It can't be true!'

He dropped to his knees, feeling all over the ground where the other man had been lying. He could not feel anything solid but the rotting floorboards of the shed. The second entity was gone, disappearing as if he had never been!

A great weight was lifted from Varden's shoulders. New life seemed to enter him. He was free now! Free to confound the plot being hatched by Merrick, a man who had once been his best friend and was now a power-seeking fiend in human guise.

But despite his newfound relief he realised he must walk with the utmost caution. Even the killing of Varden Two did not remove the shadow and stigma from himself. He was still a wanted man.

His watch told him it was two o'clock when he left the yard.

7

A Woman's Faith

Varden walked quickly, making for the address Merrick had given him as being Rhonna's. Still protected to a certain extent by his carefully-disguised face, he was not accosted or scrutinised by anyone, but nevertheless breathed a sigh of relief when he found the big block of flats and went straight up without arousing suspicion.

The door of Rhonna's flat was unlocked, so he walked in and looked round, searching for the girl. There was no sign of her in either of the two rooms, the bathroom or the kitchenette. Varden sat down to wait, impatience rising inside him.

He chose the bedroom in which to wait so that she would not run straight out again when she caught sight of him, for he was positive there would be difficulties in making her see his point of view.

He waited ten minutes before hearing her

voice outside the flat door. Then she came in, saying goodbye to another woman as she closed the front door behind her.

Varden held his breath and tried again to think of a suitable opening.

He was still thinking when she walked in from the lounge and halted dead in her tracks at sight of him. One hand went up to her mouth to check an involuntary scream, but before she could back out and slam the door he had reached her and put himself between the door and her.

That she had recognised him instantly, there was no shadow of doubt in his mind, and her first words quickly confirmed that impression.

'How dare you come here for refuge!' she breathed. 'You, a killer, coming here!' The terror showed plainly in her eyes, but she was holding herself well in hand, fearing an immediate attack.

'I'm not a killer, Rhonna,' he said, very quietly. 'If you will only give me a few minutes, I can make you see that. But it isn't why I came here. That's a secondary thing; something I hardly understand myself.'

She backed away from him, looking

round wildly for a moment. She was close to a little bedside cabinet. Before Varden could prevent it she slid the drawer out and picked up a gun from inside. Breathing hard, she levelled it at him.

'Get out of here at once!' she said. Her voice was firm now, most of the fear gone from it.

Varden shrugged and tried to smile. 'You can't kill me, Rhonna,' he said. 'Not because you wouldn't, but because you can't. That's another thing I don't follow, but it's true.'

She came towards him, step by step. 'If you don't go, I shall shoot,' she told him.

'If I could die, you'd be a murderess then,' he said. He sat down on a chair, watching her. He didn't want her to shoot because the noise would bring other people to the scene, and that would upset his plans.

'You can shoot or hand me over to the police when I've had my say,' he went, on slowly. 'I'm not armed myself, but hang on to that gun if it gives you confidence. I shan't hurt you.'

'Do you expect me to believe that after what you did to those other women?' she demanded grimly. 'I liked you once, Bob, but you're not a human being now. Get out! I'll give you two minutes' start before calling the police, and that you don't deserve.' Her eyes were hard, unrelenting in their hate.

Varden chose his words with care. He had to change her attitude in a matter of seconds. 'What would you say if I told you that before long, guided missiles would be fired on London and New York?' he began.

She stiffened fractionally, then laughed. 'I shouldn't believe you!' she snapped. 'Aren't you going to leave while you've got the chance?'

'Not till I've told you the rest of it, Rhonna. Why do you think I came here and risked my neck to see you?'

'Because you want a hideout, no doubt!'

He shook his head. 'I'm serious,' he went on. 'You've got to tell your father what I'm telling you.' He leant forward, feeling for a cigarette. Instantly the woman was on the alert.

'Only a cigarette,' he said, bringing out his case. 'May I?' He lit it slowly. She wouldn't shoot at him now, he thought. 'Merrick wants to start the war,' he said.

'The world is in a ripe state for it at the moment. What would happen, Rhonna, if a bomb landed on London? Tell me!'

She touched the tip of her tongue to her lips. The gun in her hand never faltered. 'The fools would think an enemy had committed unprovoked aggression,' she said. 'Everything's ready for instant mobilisation. Within hours the world would be flaming. But —'

'It's going to happen if you don't do something about it,' he cut in grimly.

'*I* do something?' She was genuinely surprised.

'Your father, then. He can stop a war, can't he? You've always kept on telling me so!' He drew on his cigarette with apparent calm, but inside his pulse was raging. He mustn't fail, he kept telling himself. Not now.

'Why are you telling me this?' she demanded. 'You're only trying to frighten me!'

'No, I'm not. Last time I saw you I hurt you because you hurt me with your sympathy. I didn't want it, but I didn't mean to drive you away like that. I'm no good to a woman, but I didn't mean to sneer as I did. Now I need you, not for myself, but for the safety of the world. I've just *got* to make you listen to reason!'

She stared at him closely, noting the earnestness with which he spoke. 'Can you prove what you say?' she asked.

He shrugged. 'Merrick wouldn't tell you the same,' he said flatly. 'His only object as far as I can make out is personal gain and power. He and Viki are in this together.'

'*Viki!*' she echoed. 'That woman! There's a story in the news that you visited her after committing murder the other night.'

Varden sighed. 'Rhonna, I didn't commit any murder. Do you really think I'm that kind of man? Am I?'

'W-e-l-l, I shouldn't have said so before, but —'

'I'm still not!' He sought desperately for words. 'Have you ever heard of a double entity? Can you comprehend that when something happens to a man, his soul and his being might be split in two? A sort of spiritual schizophrenia …' He stood up and walked slowly up and down the room. She was watching him.

'I didn't kill those people,' he said. 'When you saw me in hospital I swore at you, didn't I?'

She nodded dumbly, a queer expression in her green eyes.

'But I wasn't cursing you, Rhonna,' he said. 'That other being who was part of me was making me do it! I was answering his gibes, and they fitted the situation so that you thought I was talking to you.' He stopped and faced her across the gun. 'Can't you believe me, Rhonna?' he pleaded.

'Suppose I do?'

'Will you take me to your father and let him decide? You can't in all conscience let the world be plunged into war simply because the man who warns you might be a killer! This is too important for that.'

Her brows drew together. 'You say Merrick is doing this?'

He nodded. 'He can do it at a few hours' notice,' he said. 'What are you going to do about it?'

'Give me time,' she muttered uneasily. 'If only I could really believe that you didn't commit murder, Bob!'

'I've told you about the second entity.'

She shot him a shrewd glance. 'Where

is it now?'

'I killed it,' he answered simply. Then he told her how Varden Two had returned with the information he had given her. 'I just saw red and smashed it in the face with a bottle,' he ended. 'I didn't think it could be killed, but it faded out and vanished as I watched it, so it must be dead.'

'I wonder if *you* can be killed …?'

He smiled faintly. 'Don't try to find out,' he begged.

She considered briefly. 'I can't be sure,' she said. 'But I will do this: I'll fly you to Dad's place and see what he says.' She frowned. 'He's a scientist, and if he doesn't understand what you've told me about yourself, no one will.'

Varden inclined his head. 'Thank you for that,' he said quietly. 'I knew I could rely on you.'

'You can't rely on anything,' she told him. 'And I'll keep the gun, so don't be funny.'

'Quite a handful, isn't she?' He was standing in the open doorway, stroking his scarred chin, smiling with all the malice of his evil soul.

Rhonna was turning towards the door when Varden choked back a sob in his throat. She spun round, the gun in her hand moving fast. 'What are you ...?' she began, then saw the expression on his face.

'I couldn't have killed it!' he sobbed. 'Oh, God, it can't die!'

The woman eyed him narrowly.

'Go on, brother, tell her all about, me!' The jeering tones were like a whiplash to Varden. He straightened up, glaring at the nude, ugly figure now leaning over Rhonna's shoulder. She moved away, almost as if she sensed its presence.

'There's something there,' she breathed. 'Something here in this room, Bob? Is that what you mean?'

'Listen, Rhonna,' said Varden grimly. 'I'm not mad, but if I talk to it, don't take any notice. I've got to talk to it. You understand? It won't make sense to you, but ...'

'Maybe I do believe you,' she told him quietly, looking about uneasily, seeing nothing though she followed Varden's gaze to the doorway.

'You tried to kill me, Bob. That was foolish, because you know we can't die,

either of us.'

'I hoped it was possible.'

Rhonna frowned, but kept her gun trained on Varden.

'Trusting little thing, your girlfriend!'

'She has a right to be suspicious after what you did,' he snapped. 'I wouldn't blame her for shooting me on sight!'

Varden Two shook his head regretfully. *'Too bad! But I didn't come here to make small talk with you. There's a man waiting outside this building for you, Bob. A detective, and he's already sent for his friends. They'll be up here before very long. You were seen coming in. A man recognised you in spite of the make-up.'*

'Recognised me? Then the police ... Oh Lord, I can't afford that just now.'

Rhonna gave a start as she listened to Varden. 'Are the police on to you, Bob?' she demanded urgently.

'That's about it,' he grated. 'My other half says so, at any rate. What can we do?'

'Take it easy, pal! You must have a guilty conscience. I didn't say the police. I was kidding, anyway. One of our friend Merrick's private eyes is on your tail, that's

all. He is outside, though.'

Varden breathed more freely.

Rhonna said, 'If the police are after you, I suppose I'd better get you out of here somehow. Oh, Bob, I wish it hadn't come to this between us!' There were tears in her eyes as she spoke.

He felt compassion for her, even in the presence of his other personality. 'It's not the police,' he said. 'He's just told me it's one of Merrick's men. Keeping an eye on me to see I do as I'm told, no doubt.' Anger flushed his face.

'What do you mean?' she asked, puzzled.

Varden Two sneered and then turned the sneer to a grin. *'Aren't you going to tell her you're working for him?'* he said.

'No, I'm not, damn you!' snapped Varden.

Rhonna swallowed hard, but said nothing. Varden looked at her, wondering if she'd still play the same if she knew about his bargain with Merrick. She might, but he didn't want to tell her. 'Sorry,' he mumbled. 'That wasn't meant for you.'

'I guessed it,' she said, with the hint of a smile. 'Why is Merrick watching your movements?'

'She'll kick you out if you don't tell her!'

Varden ignored it. 'I can't understand,' he said slowly. 'Unless it's because he thinks your father can spoil his plans.'

She nodded shrewdly. 'You could be right,' she admitted.

Varden turned to the other man, now sitting on the edge of Rhonna's bed and studying the woman appraisingly. 'Why did you come here to tell me all this about a man on watch?' he demanded.

'Eh?' He tore his gaze from Rhonna for a moment. *'Oh, I just thought you'd like to know. I was actually coming here to play hell with you for trying to kill me, but then I realised that being watched might cramp your style with the redhead. Mustn't let the course of duty be smirched by sordid detail, must we?'*

'You're a crafty swine!' He bit his lip. 'Not you,' he added hurriedly as Rhonna glared at him in amazement.

The other man laughed. *'Mind your step!'* he advised.

Varden turned to Rhonna. 'May I use your video?' he asked.

'If you think it's safe to, by all means.

Who are you calling, Bob? Don't run any risks.'

'She's getting all fond of you, brother. Be cuddling you next. Poor lickle tootsey-wootsey Bobbie boy!'

Varden lost his already-frayed temper, hurling himself at the other man in sudden fury. Rhonna let out a gasp of fear, but Varden wasn't rushing in her direction. Incredible though it seemed to the harassed woman, she realised that an unseen fight was in progress — or, rather, a one-sided fight, only one combatant being visible.

'Is there anything I can do?' she pleaded anxiously. Varden did not answer. A hand was closed on his throat and threatened to choke him into insensibility. Only at the last moment did he tear himself free and jump clear. Then he stood away, panting and gasping as Rhonna watched in an agony of uncertainty, not knowing what was going on. Varden Two sat up straight on the bed.

'We'd better call it quits for today,' he said playfully. *'I'd hate you to be damaged at this stage! Go ahead and tell Merrick to call off his snooper!'*

Varden nodded and straightened his

collar. 'All right,' he said grimly. 'I'll square things with you another day!'

'I doubt it!' He glanced at the woman. *'Wouldn't like to go to sleep for a few minutes, would you?'* he inquired slyly.

Varden refused to answer, but went past Rhonna, drawing her through the doorway with him, keeping her close at his side as he headed for the video cabinet. 'Don't ever, ever let me drop off to sleep,' he whispered as Varden Two trailed after them a few feet in the rear.

She gave him a puzzled look, but nodded her head.

He asked for Merrick's number at Viki's flat. The screen flickered to life and showed the familiar room. Viki was there as well as Merrick. She wore a negligée and very little else.

'What did I tell you, pal? See that?' He studied the intimate little scene with a glitter of amusement. *'Quite a love-nest, isn't it?'*

Merrick blocked Viki out of sight. He frowned when he saw Varden's features. Varden had pushed Rhonna out of range of the screen

'Well?' demanded Merrick curtly. 'What

have you got to report?'

'Nothing as yet,' answered Varden tersely. 'I just thought I'd tell you I don't like being watched when I'm working. One of your men keeps hanging around. I'm busy, understand?'

Merrick made a deprecating gesture. 'I was only taking care of you in case the police got you,' he said. 'Are you on to Blake yet?'

Varden bit his lip, hearing Rhonna catch her breath. 'I'll call you when there's anything definite,' he snapped. Then he switched off the video and lifted his eyes to the red-haired woman with the gun in her hand.

'You're spying on me for Merrick, aren't you?' she said. Her voice was hard and edged.

Varden spread his hands a little helplessly. 'Don't get the wrong idea,' he told her. 'I've been honest with you except in one respect.' He paused, hesitating slightly. 'Merrick wanted me to find out what your father could do to stop the war. I told him I wouldn't do it, and I meant it.'

'Is that true? You're being honest with

me?' There was an anxious ring to her words, as if she prayed he would not let her down. Varden nodded firmly, catching the eye of the other man as he stood beside her. Varden Two winked in a knowing fashion.

'It's perfectly true,' Varden insisted. 'If you were on the run from the police, would you bother to spy on people for another man's benefit?'

'All right,' she said, relieved. 'We'd better go now. Is — is that other thing around still?'

'Yes, I'm afraid he is.'

'Don't worry about me, brother. I'm content to stay where I am for the time being. Later on, I might make other plans. But you go right ahead with the lady. And don't forget to come through with the dope, either. If you slip, I'll be right there beside you, understand?'

Varden nodded. He said nothing, for fear of starting an unwanted train of thought in Rhonna's mind.

Rhonna said, 'Bob, if you're ready, we'll go.'

'Let's,' he said. 'Where to?'

'You'll see.' She glanced at the gun in her hand, then picked up a light coat and dropped it over her arm — covering the gun but still leaving it usable if Varden turned killer. He watched her with mingled amusement and hurt. She still didn't trust him entirely.

The other Varden strolled to the front door of the flat in a leisurely manner. Then he leant against the jamb and barred the way as Varden made to leave. Varden stopped abruptly.

'Well?' he demanded.

'I just want to impress on you what I've already said. Oh, and by the way, I discovered why Merrick's so anxious to have a war. He's deep in the armament business. That's strictly for your own information, but I thought you'd like to know.'

'Thanks!' Varden was sceptical of the being's intention, but accepted it for what it was worth. Rhonna made no comment, but followed him closely and quickly as he stepped past the figure of the leaning entity.

'Up in the lift,' she said. 'To the roof: I have a plane of my own up there.'

The other Varden watched them go, a cynical smile on his lips.

111

8

Mental Probe

Viki Rochelle stretched her arms luxuriously, smiling at Merrick as he brought her a drink and perched himself on the settee beside her.

'You know, darling,' she murmured huskily, 'you're very sweet and very important to me, but I'll be glad when all this is over and we can really enjoy the fruits of what we're doing.' She took the glass he offered and raised her mouth for the kiss that went with it.

'Viki,' he whispered intensely, 'it's as much for you as for myself. We shall have the world at our feet before long, and then we can dictate our own terms.' He paced the floor, an odd expression on his fleshy face. 'And when it's all over, I shall finish off Varden,' he added, smiling grimly.

Viki looked worried for a moment. 'It can't be true about there being two of him,

112

can it?' she said. 'It gives me the creeps when I remember the other night.'

Merrick waved a podgy hand. 'Rubbish, of course!' He bent forward, smiling.

It was then that the video screen flickered to life and Varden came through from Rhonna's flat. When the conversation was over, Viki was even more worried than before. Her nerves were on edge and she grew more restless. She and Merrick began snapping at each other over trivialities. In the end, he smoothed her down, but she was still disgruntled.

Neither of them saw the figure of Varden's other entity come in and take a seat at the writing desk. Viki glanced round uneasily, sensing something in the atmosphere, but there was nothing visible to her eyes. She shivered and snuggled more deeply on the settee, huddling down so that Merrick shot her a curious look.

'You cold or something?' he inquired impatiently. 'Better go and dress if you are.' He walked about restlessly.

'What a way to appreciate a lady's charm!' murmured Varden, shaking his head as if scandalised. But they took no notice of him.

'I'm all right,' said Viki. 'It's just ... Oh, I don't know!' She got up and poured herself another drink, double the size of her last. Her hands were none too steady.

Merrick grinned at her. 'You'll feel better when we fly to the yacht,' he said quietly. 'All I'm waiting for is Varden to make his report. Then we can go ahead. Think of it, honey! War! A war of our own creation, with all the loot and profit that belongs to war. My contracts are bigger than ever, and even if war eventually blocks the raw materials from reaching us, we shall clear a thousand million at the least!' His eyes were gleaming greedily as he spoke.

The Varden by the desk smiled slowly and thoughtfully. He would have liked to have discussed the question with Merrick, but was seriously handicapped in that respect. There was no way of getting into direct communication as far as he could see. Then he wondered, looking at the clean sheet of blotting paper on the desk.

Viki was saying, 'You're sure no one can give us away? The yacht. I mean ... Suppose they discovered the launching gear?' Her voice was harsh with worry. Merrick spun round on her almost savagely.

'For heaven's sake!' he snapped. 'There isn't any danger! Why the devil should anyone suspect a cruising yacht in the Atlantic Ocean? My dear girl, be your age!'

Varden was scribbling with a pencil, listening as he wrote. If he could get rid of whiskey, there didn't seem to be any reason why he shouldn't write messages, he thought with amusement. When he had finished to his satisfaction, he picked up the blotter and took it across to Merrick, thrusting it into the man's hand. Merrick gave a yell of dismay and horror. Viki screamed. But the moment Merrick had recovered his balance he saw that there was scrawly writing on the blotter. The first few words riveted his attention, and in spite of his astonishment and fear be began to read the message through.

'Shut up, Viki!' he snarled. 'Listen: *I am Varden. You can't see me, but I'm real for all that. I'm not the other Varden who's now with the Blake girl, but I feel we should get together on this war question. Varden means to double-cross you and is on his way to Blake with the girl. If you want to get in with a rush, I should fire those projectiles as soon as you can.*

'Do you hear that, Viki?' His tone was scared as he peered round the room uneasily. 'This — this was written in here!'

Varden's entity drifted round behind Viki where she cowered on the settee, terrified. He stroked her hair, wondering if she could feel him. She may have sensed his presence, but no more.

Merrick thrust his hands in his pockets, striking a pose of courage which he did not feel. 'Er — Varden,' he said firmly. 'Is this true? Can't you speak to me, man?'

Silence. Varden grinned and studied the big man's face. He wished he could do something really frightening. However, by coming here like this he had learnt something fresh, and he had also jogged Merrick considerably.

Merrick frowned. 'All right,' he said loudly. 'If you can't make me hear, I'm thanking you for this information. If it interests you, we are leaving shortly for the projectile base. That is all you need to know. Later on, we may be able to take you into partnership when things get going.' Merrick beamed a big business smile, tossing it round the room in all directions, hoping it would land.

Varden smirked. *'You poor sap,'* he said. *'Do you imagine I'll swallow that? When you begin, friend, I'll take up where you leave off!'*

Merrick rubbed his hands together. 'Good!' he said with a hearty chuckle. 'I'm glad you called, Varden, You've put us on our guard. Much obliged to you!' He waved his hand in dismissal, then turned to Viki. 'Go and dress, my dear,' he said. 'I think we will be off. Hurry now!'

Viki glanced round with frightened eyes, then ran from the room. Varden decided she might be worth following.

Merrick was alone, though he could not be sure on that point. He helped himself to a drink and a cigarette, scowling and chewing his lower lip. So the fool meant to double-cross him, did he? Well, there was a simple way of beating him at that! Once the war was started, it would be much more difficult to stop — even if Blake did have the means. Merrick racked his brains, but could think of no possible way in which one man could prevent a war by scientific methods. The whole idea was ridiculous, he told himself, yet there was little conviction in his mind.

Viki slipped the negligée from her shoulders and turned to study her reflection in the glass. She gulped and gave a yell of dismay as Varden wrote something on the mirror with lipstick. She couldn't even see the lipstick itself, because, for some reason that even Varden's second entity did not understand, things were not always visible to other people when he picked them up. He watched vindictively as the woman ran and hid on the other side of the bed.

At last Merrick himself came in, hurrying Viki impatiently. Within five minutes they were going up in the lift to the roof, where Merrick's personal jet helicopter was parked.

★　★　★

The small, fast machine bearing Rhonna and Varden winged its way north across the drowsy summer countryside. The woman handled her aircraft expertly, so that Varden was reminded of his own flying days, now finished. He was troubled, too, by recurring headaches and a growing certainty that his eyesight was not as good as it had been when he left the hospital. But he said nothing to Rhonna about it. Better to get this other affair settled before bringing up his own particular worries. And he could not, in any event, return to the fat little doctor with rimless glasses at the hospital. There were times when he forgot he was a wanted man, but this was not one of them.

Rhonna said little during the flight. Once, when Varden asked her again where they were going, she told him to wait and see. It was plain that although she would have liked to, she could not place all her trust in this man. He swallowed the hurt, but kept his temper.

Two hours' swift flying brought them to the Highland country of Scotland, bare and heather-clad, with occasional small farms dotted here and there in the dales, a country that had not changed as much as England.

She took the plane down in a perpendicular drop, landing it neatly and without fuss alongside the buildings of a somewhat larger farm than most, a place without neighbours closer than several miles across the hills.

'Here we are,' she said quietly. 'You can get out now — and remember, I still have you covered with this!' She jerked the little gun in her hand.

Varden grinned. 'You won't have to use it,' he said. 'I'm in your hands now, and when your father hears what you have to tell him, he'll see the wisdom of acting quickly.'

'I hope so, for your sake,' she told him enigmatically.

They left the jet-powered 'copter and walked quickly to the farmhouse fifty yards away. Before they reached it, the front door opened and a man stepped out into the clear sunlight. His hair was almost white. He was smallish, a little bent about the shoulders, and none-too-tidily-dressed, but his eyes lit up when he saw Rhonna coming.

Varden shot her a sidelong glance, seeing the answering warmth in her eyes, the unconscious quickening of her step so that she almost outdistanced him. 'Dad!' she said. 'Dad, is it all right? Is everything all right?'

He was a tired-looking man, past middle

age, with a lot of work and personal struggle behind those weary eyes of his. Varden liked him on sight. He realised that this was the first time he'd met Rhonna's father. In the old days before the crash he hadn't known her long enough to get as far as meeting Dad; and since then ... well, there hadn't been time.

Blake was peering at him curiously, fumbling his hands in the side pockets of his coat, waiting. Rhonna turned and made a comprehensive gesture with her gun. Blake didn't seem to have noticed the gun till then. He gave a start of surprise.

'Don't worry,' said Rhonna, smiling a little. 'He's a wanted man, but I don't think he did it. There's something you can help us with, Dad. And something even more important, too, that you've got to get hold of.'

Blake surveyed Varden with a calculating stare that was partly friendly and partly hostile.

'You'd both better come indoors,' he said. 'I'll send one of the men to put the plane under cover.'

Varden decided he was going to like

Blake. He walked in behind him, with Rhonna bringing up the rear. The inside of the house was like that of any other remote farm, plain and comfortably furnished. Blake closed the door as his daughter entered, then waved Varden to a chair.

'Make yourself at home,' he said. He glanced at Rhonna. 'I think I can trust my daughter's choice of friends.'

'I'm Robert Varden. I didn't come here to escape the law, Mr. Blake, but because you've got to listen to something I have to say, something about war …'

Blake showed no immediate reaction. Rhonna went close to her father's side. 'He means it, Dad,' she said. 'A man by the name of Merrick is aiming to start the war on his own. Bob says that if you can prevent it you must act now.'

Blake eyed Varden closely. 'Stay here,' he said. 'I'll have a talk with Rhonna about it.' He paused. Then: 'Don't run away; there isn't any need. If you're honest, you're with friends.'

Varden smiled gratefully. Blake and Rhonna went into a second room and closed the door. He could hear their voices for several minutes before Blake returned alone. He seemed more interested in Varden now.

'I've been hearing about your double being,' he said slowly. 'Will you place yourself in my hands?'

'You can do what you like if you'll get rid of that awful killer that's part of me,' Varden answered.

Blake nodded. 'Rhonna believes your story,' he said. 'I want to check it myself. Come with me, will you?'

Varden followed him from the room, through a second one, to a flight of steps down which they walked. The steps were broad concrete ones, well lighted. From far below came the hum of machinery. Puzzled, Varden wondered where the scientist was taking him; wondered, too, why a man like Blake should bury himself in the Highlands. It only dawned on him slowly that he was being taken to a great underground laboratory and workshop. But he saw little of it at that stage.

Blake led him through a steel door to a small, office-like room. 'Sit down,' he said quietly.

Varden glanced apprehensively as the scientist wheeled a trolley towards the chair in which he sat. 'What's this in aid of?' he demanded uneasily, as the man placed a metal plate on his skull and put a pistol-grip attachment in his hand.

Blake smiled. 'Nothing to be afraid of,' he assured him. 'I want to check this story you've been telling Rhonna. And it might help to solve your other problem, too. You can trust me.' He made some adjustments to some electrical apparatus on the trolley. 'Now, I want you to let your mind relax,' he said, peering into Varden's eyes.

Panic gripped him. 'Don't you put me to sleep!' he said.

Blake shook his head. 'Rhonna told me about that. All you have to do is relax. You won't sleep, but I shall get all the information I want without your knowing.'

Varden could hardly believe his ears. He watched as Blake put on a pair of headphones and flicked a switch, his eyes on a dial, the needle of which was moving spasmodically.

'Relax!' said Blake sharply.

Varden closed his eyes, striving to make

his mind a blank. Then suddenly he felt a probe working deep in his brain. It was as if something hard and metallic was feeling its way through his skull, seeking and questing blindly. Queer thoughts rose in his mind, unbidden, strange to him. He felt as if he was floating on a calm sea, yet was perfectly well aware of his surroundings.

He opened his eyes and watched the face of the scientist. It was intent, concentrated. More thoughts passed through his mind. He visualised the second Varden, a naked figure with devil's eyes and a leering grin; Viki in all her seductiveness; Merrick with his big business pomposity and phoney heartiness. He thought of a thousand tiny details relating to his life during the past few days, and not one of them did he call up consciously from the dimness of his mind.

At last Blake gave a satisfied nod. He switched off the apparatus, smiling at Varden with friendly eyes as he lifted the plate off his skull and relieved him of the pistol-grip gadget.

'You're all right,' he said, as if relieved. 'You're not a murderer, Varden, but that other entity that belongs to you is.'

Varden gulped uncomfortably and felt for a cigarette. 'How did you work all that out?' he inquired.

Blake smiled tiredly. 'Oh, that? Measured electrical impulses applied to the brain tissue show reactions on the dial,' he explained. 'I can listen in to the static reflexes resulting and form my own opinion. Various differing impulses bring up a whole procession of thoughts in your mind, and from them I can make a mental picture of your recent activities. It's simple really, though it sounds a bit complicated at first.'

Varden grunted. 'You're telling me!' he said. 'So I'm not a killer, eh? Well, I knew that, but it's good to have it confirmed by an outside source.' He broke off. 'Er — is there any chance of getting rid of my other half before he does any more damage?' He watched Blake anxiously, searching his face for hope of redemption.

But Blake shook his head regretfully. 'Not that I know of,' he admitted. 'We may think of something later on, but at the moment your second entity is a permanent attachment.' He took a turn round the office, hands behind his back, frowning. 'The thing that worries me is how to keep the man intangible and let you sleep at the same time. Mind you, I can keep you awake for a year if I want to, but that's no real solution. However ... '

Varden grunted. He was dog-tired and his eyelids were heavy, but he didn't want to sleep. He daren't! Blake seemed to understand. He gave Varden a glass of some drug which immediately livened him up, driving all desire to sleep away.

'That'll keep you going for six hours,' Blake told him. 'Now we'll hunt out Rhonna.' He sounded almost cheerful now.

In a large, artificially-lighted workshop, a dozen young men were engaged in working on some huge piece of mechanism foreign to Varden. Rhonna was with them, looking on and occasionally speaking to one or other of them.

'What is it?' asked Varden, pointing to the towering machine.

Blake smiled, but only shook his head. Then: 'It can prevent a war from developing; or cause such chaos as the world has never seen,' he replied.

Rhonna joined them, and they entered a comfortable room which was obviously Blake's own study. The scientist nodded to his daughter. 'He's all right,' he said quietly. 'Nothing wrong with his motives in coming here, though at one time he was ready to work against us through pressure being brought to bear on him.

She nodded soberly. 'Merrick,' she mused. 'I'm glad, Bob. Glad you made me see sense, I mean.'

'What else can I do now you've accepted me?' he wanted to know.

Blake said, 'Can you find out where this launching base is? If you can, we can immobilise it without using our full output and so causing chaos in other places. That's only for an emergency.'

Varden didn't understand, but said, 'I can try. My other half may have found out by this time; or I may be able to get it from Merrick myself.'

Rhonna was on her feet at once. 'I'll fly you back to London,' she said. 'Merrick won't act till he has your report.' She smiled. 'It's all right; Dad discovered that himself. Merrick still thinks you're working for him. Very well: give him something to go on with! But get the location of that launching base.'

Varden grinned broadly. It hurt his face, but was worth it. 'Come on then!' he said. "Now we're getting somewhere!'

9

Fugitive

Back in London, Rhonna dropped the helicopter deftly on the roof of her own apartment block.

'It'll be here for when we come back,' she said.

Varden looked at her sharply. 'You're staying right here,' he told her. 'This is my game from now on!'

She tried to protest, but knew it was useless. 'I'll be all right,' he promised. 'The moment I get what we want, I'll come running, so be ready for the leap.'

She stood in front of him quickly. 'Be careful, Bob,' she pleaded. 'I — I don't want anything to happen to you now.'

He looked down at her in the evening twilight. Suddenly he wanted to take her in his arms, but something stopped him. A shadow seemed to cross his eyes, dimming the appeal of her face. If his sight went ... He turned quickly without even touching her hands, not even glancing over his shoulder as he made for the penthouse lift.

No one recognised him as he went through the streets to Viki's place. At one corner he caught sight of a newscast screen that was showing a picture of his own face. He realised with a shock that it must be a photograph of himself taken in the morgue before he cheated death and walked out. It left him with a nasty sensation of unreality as he hurried on. But his made-up features still offered disguise of a kind.

On purpose he went up the fire escape to Viki's flat, not wanting to run any risks, and wishing to take the woman by surprise if he could. It might strengthen his hand, though he was not yet sure what approach to make.

There was no one in the lounge when he entered through the window. He could smell perfume and the tang of whiskey. He walked through to the bedroom, moving on silent feet.

'I was waiting for you, brother! How goes it?'

Varden halted abruptly, his heart missing

a beat. Then he saw the man, lying on the big double bed with his fingers laced at the back of his neck. Some of Viki's clothes were strewn about the floor as if she had dressed in a hurry. His gaze took in the scrawled words on the mirror.

'So they've gone, have they?' he bit out grimly. 'What are you hanging about for?'

'To see if you'd come back, or if I'd have to fetch you.'

Varden stared at him in blind hatred. 'I said I'd be back, and I've kept my word!'

Varden the Naked swung his legs to the ground and strolled to the uncurtained window, glancing out. When he turned he was grinning wickedly. *'So I see,'* he murmured. *'A pity you weren't here to see them go, Bob. They were more or less on fighting terms by then! I scared the living daylights out of little Viki, and Merrick wasn't much better off. Then they beat it for the high seas!'*

Varden frowned incredulously. 'You mean they've run off without waiting for me?' he blurted.

Varden Two nodded thoughtfully. *'I imagine they didn't think it necessary to hang around any longer,'* he said.

'How long have they been gone?'

'Long enough to get there.'

'Where, blast you!'

'The yacht, somewhere in the Atlantic from what I gathered.' He came away from the window, making for the lounge. *'If I were you, brother, I wouldn't take on so,'* he advised. *'Just let it ride. The war's about due to begin, and I reckon you're a lot too late to influence it one way or the other by now. You've shot your bolt.'*

Varden stiffened, fighting to curb the outburst that would send him thrashing at this grinning creature with the insolent voice. Instead he went into the lounge, hunting round for a possible clue. If only he knew the whereabouts of the yacht! It was then that he found the blotter with the writing on it. He recognised his own handwriting, but knew he had not penned the words.

Varden swung round, his last reserve of patience gone. He hurled himself forward in a savage onslaught, his fist striking his enemy on the temple. Then they were tangling briskly on the floor, weaving and diving and smashing at each other. Once,

Varden thought he was going out, but recovered and landed a blow that made the other man fade for a moment or two.

'You're asking for trouble, Bob!'

He crouched, teeth bared. 'I'll kill you if it's the last thing I ever do!' he grated, darting in again.

Varden Two ducked. Varden crashed against a desk and sobbed with pain.

'Don't forget what happens when you lose your senses!' He picked up a heavy vase and hurled it. Varden rolled away as it shattered against the wall. Then he came up more cautiously. In a sudden movement that took his opponent off-balance, he fixed his hand on the other man's throat and squeezed and squeezed till blood was pounding in his own temples with the exertion.

Varden Two began to go limp, sagging to the floor in a heap. Varden watched him eagerly, waiting for his body to disappear. A second or two more would have done it. Then the door burst open and uniformed men poured through, filling the lounge and rushing Varden, hurling him away so that he lost his grip on his other entity. Varden

Two no longer faded.

'All right, boys!' yelled a big patrolman. 'Get him down to the car! He won't slip us this time!'

Varden was roughly handled, bundled out of the flat and down to the entrance foyer in the lift. Varden Two rode with them, content now to watch his counterpart's discomfort, content to laugh tauntingly in the knowledge that whatever they did they could not kill him.

Varden sat in the lift between two men. There were handcuffs on his wrists and steely fingers bit the flesh of his arms. They were taking no chances with him this time.

Out in the foyer he came under the hostile and curious eyes of a growing crowd who shouted for his blood. He was the Killer!

A large black gyro-car was parked at the curb. He was pushed in, with men all round him. More handcuffs were put on his wrists, fastening him to two of the policemen. And all the time he was thinking: they can't kill me; I don't belong in this time at all; I belong in a plane over the Atlantic in a storm; they can't kill me because I don't exist anymore.

Looking up through the transparent roof of the car, he saw the grinning face of his other self, staring back at him. He screamed several times before one of the men in the car smashed his mouth with a knotted fist.

The car sped swiftly through the heart of the city. Varden tried not to look up at the entity on the roof, riding like a fiend in triumph. He asked the nearest patrolman how they'd caught up with him. He'd been recognised coming up the fire escape by someone in one of the other flats.

The bomb came down as the car was streaking round a corner. For one instant, the life of London was its own tumbled tangle of movement and noise. Then the bomb fell.

Varden saw a great gout of orange and violet flame shoot skywards and blossom in a gigantic flower of death. Heat and blast seemed to catch him in a tearing grasp. He heard men screaming around him, saw their blood flowing from ears and mouths. The gyro-car was lifted up and hurled through the air, a twisted mass of metal. Fire enveloped him in its searing breath, and the stench of burning flesh turned him sick. As the shattered car sailed upwards, he saw blocks of buildings melt into rubble, erupting torn and broken bodies in the worst disaster his mind could comprehend. Then the gyro-car smashed against the earth again, one tiny pile of wreckage among a million others.

Pain tore his body to fragments, he went blind, and the dark was glowing with fire, wracked with the agony of hell. Then the dark was no longer red but black. He was conscious of no more pain, only stillness. And, inside himself, he laughed horribly.

★ ★ ★

Varden opened his eyes to see a bright red glow all round him. He wondered about it for a minute or two, then knew it was fire.

He struggled up weakly, peering round. There had been a lot of men in that car, he remembered. They were still around him — parts of them. The handcuffs were gone from his wrists. He saw a moist, glistening red thing that had been a man's face close to his shoulder. One of the handcuffs was still attached to someone's wrist … only the wrist wasn't fixed to a body anymore.

Shuddering violently, he clawed his way out through a hole in the side of the car. There was death and carnage wherever he looked. And fire. For the first time, he remembered to examine himself. His clothes hung in scorched shreds from his frame, and there was soot on his skin — but no sign of burns.

Varden stood among the rubble of shattered concrete and laughed with hideous abandon. God, why couldn't he die? He started to work his way to where the pavement had once been. There were only jumbled piles of masonry now. A ghastly loneliness enveloped him. Even to the end of the world, he would walk in this dreadful immunity, he thought. Presently he stopped and sank down on a pile of rubble, to get a grip on himself and think more clearly. No more voices cried from the debris; there was nothing alive to cry now. He looked down at his feet, finding them planted on the naked body of a man. Blast had stripped it of skin, stripped it of everything but its barest outline.

The heat of the blazing fire reminded him that, although he was immortal he could still feel pain. He got to his feet and stared round, wondering which direction to take, how to get out of this hell that was Merrick's creation.

And then he remembered Rhonna, and a cold dread settled on his heart like an icy clamp. If she'd been killed ...

He started running, panic riding on his shoulder when he thought of the woman with red hair and freckles. She couldn't die! She mustn't be dead! More than anything else, he wanted her to live. He'd be content to endure a living hell of his own for that. But what chance could she have stood? What earthly chance did anything normal stand in that blasting, tearing burst?

When he reached what he thought had been the block in which Rhonna lived, he found only rubble. And more death. He searched with frantic speed, handling the shattered flesh of the dead in an effort to find out whether Rhonna was among them. But it was a hopeless task. He knew she couldn't have lived in this holocaust of slaughter. He covered his eyes with his hands and sat very still, broken sobs vibrating his frame.

The sound of voices brought his head up sharply, voices among the dead. The dead can't speak, he thought dully. But it was not the dead who spoke. He saw rescue workers, police, troops. They came from beyond the splintered buildings and the piles of rubble. Not everyone could be dead in London. That was a funny thing, he thought. He laughed, and someone grabbed his arm.

'Are there any more alive?' asked a patrolman urgently. 'How did you get away with it?'

Varden peered at him blankly. His eyesight was worse now. 'I don't know,' he said. 'I'm immortal. There's another of me somewhere, but you'll never find him.'

People pressed round him — curiously, pityingly. Some shook their heads. He was led back through the rubble and death to a parked helicopter rescue plane. A pale-faced girl was in it, laying out dressings and drugs on a built-in cabinet top. Her hands were unsteady as she worked.

'Here you are, miss,' someone said. 'First casualty. Bomb-shocked. Better dope him up and keep him quiet.'

She put Varden on a bunk. The plane was as big as a troop carrier, he realised. But he didn't want any dope. He mustn't sleep, whatever happened; even now, when it didn't matter anymore.

The girl was young and badly shaken. 'Lie still,' she told him. 'You'll be all right.'

'What'll happen now?' he asked.

'What do you think?' Her eyes blazed for a moment. 'We shan't stand for an attack like this! The Air Force is already on the move. If they want war, they'll get it!'

'They didn't start it!' he said desperately. 'Merrick did that. Don't you understand? You've got to stop them!'

A look of comprehension crossed her face. 'Of course,' she said gently. 'Lie still and rest now. There's nothing to worry about.' She was coming towards him with a hypodermic.

'Oh, you fool, you fool!' he gasped. 'You're as blind as the rest of them!' He swung himself off the bunk and rushed her. She screamed and cowered. He didn't have to hit her. Then he was outside the plane again, staring round wildly. More aircraft were dropping from the sky, landing all over the city in the faint hope of finding life. He joined the groups of rescue workers, barely noticed among them. If he could get hold of a plane ... he thought. He must. An Air Force machine dropped down nearby. An officer with a strained white face stepped out, calling something to the men as he approached. Varden wondered if he could make it.

'All civilian planes being commandeered,' someone said quietly. 'By God, we'll give 'em hell for this! Joe, take a look at this kid I've just found.'

Joe looked and shuddered. Varden moved on hurriedly. He had seen worse sights than that in the past few minutes. Some of the planes that hovered overhead carried floodlights on their undersides, lighting the scene in all its horror. Several more planes moved aimlessly to and fro, searching. One stayed over Varden and the group he was with for a full minute. A patrolman waved to it, yelling for it to land. They needed all the help they could get.

Varden left the group and followed it. There were no rescue workers close to where it was landing. A few policemen moved about, commandeering other planes on Air Force orders. If Varden could get in ahead ... He hurried.

Someone left the plane as he approached. Four patrolmen came up from the opposite side, calling to the pilot. Varden broke into a stumbling run. He could beat them yet! He was close to the pilot now, ready to strike. He must have that plane! He must reach Blake!

'Bob! Thank God! Quickly!' The pilot seized him by the arm as he tensed himself to fight. He saw Rhonna's face in the flickering fire glow, the glaring floods from above. The freckles stood out more sharply. They raced for the plane, the police on their heels. Varden pushed Rhonna in front of him. She'd left the engine running. As she settled at the controls, he turned to meet the first attack. There was cold hate inside him, tightening his stomach. He heard the plane lift a little. Then a man was on him, trying to stop him as he turned to jump for the plane. He lashed out with all his strength. More men closed in, wild to prevent what they thought was looting. Varden crashed a fist into the nearest face, blanking it out. Someone made a grab at his arm, but the remains of his jacket tore loose. He grasped the edge of the plane door as Rhonna yelled at him. Then he scrambled in as she lifted the craft off the ground. He felt her lean over and haul him in, then collapsed in a heap on the floor. When he pulled himself together, they were zooming upwards in a perpendicular rise.

10

The Switch is Thrown

'They were going to fill me up with dope,' he said grimly. 'I had to run for it. The police had me before that; I was recognised. They were all killed when the bomb fell. It was horrible.'

She nodded. 'I couldn't just sit around waiting for you, Bob. I flew south a bit, stooging around to take my mind off things. Lucky I did, because the plane was well away from town when the bomb fell. I was on my way back, and saw it.'

'You must have thought I'd be finished,' he murmured.

She seemed surprised. 'You told me you couldn't be killed, so I searched and searched. It was almost hopeless, then I saw you and landed.'

'And now what?' His voice was grave. 'Merrick's had his way. Can your father prevent it going further?'

The plane sped on swiftly through the night, heading north.

'There's a drastic cure,' she said. 'No use using local interference after this. The whole world's already bubbling with war.' She paused. 'I hope we reach the farm in time.'

He shot her a puzzled glance, not understanding. In the moonlight, he saw many other aircraft: some converging on London, others gathering on Air Force fields. Rhonna's face was grim as she watched.

They landed at the farm, to find Blake in the underground laboratory and workshop. He and his assistants were working feverishly to complete their equipment. A last-minute hitch meant a few more hours before the apparatus was ready.

'For twenty years I've slaved on this,' he said, as Rhonna and Varden joined him. 'And now it's almost too late!' His eyes were tired, and he looked as if he had not slept for weeks.

'You can't delay any longer, Dad,' she answered. 'Isn't there anything we can do?'

He shook his head. Then: 'You can keep an eye on the screens if you like. Keep us up to date with developments.' He turned to

Varden. 'This is all strange to you, naturally, but we do know what we're doing. I must leave you with Rhonna now. There's so little time.' He moved away quickly.

She touched Varden's arm. 'Come to the screen room,' she said. He followed her submissively, curious at all he saw.

The screen room proved to be a darkened chamber, on the walls of which were numbers of video screens, each with its control panel. 'Covers the world at a glance,' Rhonna said swiftly, sitting at one of the sets and switching on. Varden watched. Rhonna turned knobs, and he found himself staring at a massed flight of heavy bombers lined up for take-off on some unnamed airfield in the dark of night. Men hurried here and there, their faces seen briefly in the glare of arc-lights, grim and hard.

Rhonna tuned into a different scene. At some location on the earth, a fleet appeared, surging through the water at full speed. She jotted something down on a pad beside her, then again changed the picture of war preparation. Tanks, great rumbling monsters of destruction, moved swiftly over a barren plain, their colours

147

easily recognisable.

Varden sat down at another set, following the woman's example. For a time they worked as a team. He had got the hang of it now. Between them, they covered the civilised world on the various sets, making notes of mobilised forces and the direction in which they were moving.

Rhonna gave a tired little sigh. 'In a few hours' time, the first clashes will begin,' she said. 'If only we can be ready by then! Oh, Bob, if only Dad can do it!'

Varden smiled. 'I don't know what he's going to do,' he said quietly. 'But I hope so, too. Lord, but I'm tired.'

'I'll get you another dose of stimulant,' she told him. 'Take these reports to the workshop.'

He found Blake still hard at work making fine adjustments to a maze of crystal threads in a large opalescent dome.

'The forces are gathering,' he said. 'Rhonna reckons a few more hours will bring them together in the first onslaught. Will you be ready by then?'

Blake nodded quickly. 'Hope so,' he grunted. 'There's nothing you can do in here, Bob, so take it easy.' He eyed him with sudden friendliness. 'Keep Rhonna amused and take her mind off what's going on, there's a good chap.'

Varden grinned, but the tiredness increased inside him, and he knew his eyes were worse now. For a moment he saw two of Blake, then the man was a hazy outline. Slowly, his vision cleared. A sick apprehension filled him. He was going blind again, and there wasn't time to do much about it now. He wondered vaguely if the second entity would go blind at the same time; that was something he'd never asked it about. And where was it, anyway? Had it withstood the blast of the bomb just as he himself had? He turned away and found Rhonna waiting for him with another dose of the stimulant Blake had given him before. His tiredness slipped from him like a discarded coat when he took it.

'Bless you,' he said, with a smile.

The screens showed breaking day or coming night, according to which part of the world they were tuned in on. And the vast fleets of ships, bombers, fighters, tanks and marching armies were rolling together in a dozen fields of war.

Varden and Rhonna viewed the scene soberly. Already the first bombing raids were in progress, and as yet there was no sign that Blake was finished. He worked on tirelessly, assistants backing him up to the limit of endurance.

'If your father can halt all this before it really develops, why didn't he give his secret to the government?' asked Varden.

Rhonna pushed the copper coloured hair from her forehead with a weary gesture. 'Because he was afraid,' she replied. 'He feared it would be used or stolen by our enemies. When he did approach them with the idea in the first place, they jeered.' Her eyes lit up with an imp of accusation. 'You jeered, too, Bob, along with everyone else. No one man could stop a war!'

'I still can't believe it,' he answered gravely.

'You will,' she said firmly. 'I've known my father a long time, and he doesn't make statements that can't be proved.' She paused, staring angrily at a picture of rank on rank of alien war machines moving fast across a country somewhere in Europe.

'When he throws the switches, all this will stop,' she added.

Varden watched her face for a moment. 'I wish I could be as positive,' he murmured. 'Tell me, Rhonna, can a man exist in another time plane without realising it?'

She frowned. 'You're worried about yourself, aren't you?'

'I don't belong to all this,' he said flatly. 'I crashed a plane seventeen years ago. That's where I probably died, only I didn't know it.' He stared at her with sudden intensity. 'Am I real to you?' he demanded. 'I'm not a normal man like your father, or those others who died in London. They were flesh and blood, they could die and suffer pain and find release in death. I can't!'

She came and stood beside him, looking up into his scarred face. 'Do you want to die?' she whispered. 'You're real to me, Bob. You're older and harder, but you're real enough.' Her eyes were so grave and beseeching that he turned away, not daring to translate their message, because it couldn't be true and mustn't happen if it was.

'You didn't die seventeen years ago,' she said. 'I saw you alive; I'm still seeing you

151

alive. Don't you understand?'

'No!' His voice sharpened as he closed his mind to what was happening. 'You're as much a nightmare as everything else! You're no more real than Viki or the other part of me or Merrick or all this!' He waved his arm. Suddenly he gripped her shoulders, turning her towards him fiercely. 'I'm going blind again!' he grated. 'Blind and unkillable! Could anything be worse?'

Before she could answer Blake came in, his eyes bright. 'It's done!' he said quietly. 'Do you hear, Rhonna? We can get to work at last.'

Varden swung round, his own troubles forgotten. He had difficulty in focusing on the scientist. There was a cloud across his vision, a cloud that grew dark then light then dark again before fading altogether.

Rhonna seized his arm and hustled him out of the screen room as her father led the way. The hum of machinery was loud in the confined space of the underground workshop. An atmosphere of tension seemed to grip all those present, from Blake himself to Varden, an outsider in the place.

Blake moved across to a switchboard

facing the dome Varden had noticed before. Inside it were uncountable fibres, all arranged in some incomprehensible order beyond his understanding. The men who had worked with Blake gathered in a group, eyes on their leader in his hour of triumph.

Blake put a hand up and reached for a switch, drawing it down in a clean, faultless movement. Every eye was fixed on the big opalescent dome. The whine of machinery rose in pitch. The dome itself came to life, the fibres within it glowing with some queer force of their own.

And Rhonna was clutching Varden's arm without knowing she did it, her whole concentration on the dome. He found himself as much enthralled as anyone else then was conscious of movement behind him. Tearing his gaze away from the glowing interior of the dome, he glanced over his shoulder.

'*Glad I didn't miss this bit,*' murmured the other Varden. '*What's the old boy got there, anyway?*'

★ ★ ★

The atomic-engined yacht *Cherokee* surged through the oiling swell of the Atlantic Ocean, cruising on a predetermined course. Her skipper was talking to his second-in-command in the wheelhouse, while the latter studied a chart with an earnest expression on his darkly saturnine features.

'The moment the owner gives the word,' said the skipper, 'we lay off for New York. After that, it's up to him, but I don't mind betting we make out nicely on the deal.'

The other man nodded wordlessly. Then Merrick came in. 'Everything all right?' he inquired briskly. 'We can't get the first results in for half an hour or so. Keep her as she is, cruising.'

The skipper touched his cap obediently. 'You reckon the projectiles landed accurately?' he asked.

Merrick gave a grunt. 'I never make mistakes!' he said. 'Your job is to obey orders, nothing more.'

The skipper made no comment, but his mouth tightened a little. Merrick departed, smiling grimly to himself. Things were going to hum before long, he thought. He felt a sense of gratitude towards that second personality of Varden's that had warned him of the double-crossing. He still experienced a shudder when he remembered how the unseen being had moved in Viki's flat, writing things and upsetting their nerves. However, it had all turned out for the best, he reflected.

He went below and joined Viki in the main saloon. She was feeling better now after her harrowing experience in London.

Back in the charthouse, the skipper looked at his second-in-command with a sour grin. 'Damn the man!' he grunted. 'If he didn't have a hold on us, I swear we'd leave him flat!'

The other man nodded and bent over the charts. He did not see the naked figure at his elbow as he marked off their position on the chart. The naked figure chuckled to himself, made sure he knew what he wanted to know, then drifted off again.

After a brief glance into the main saloon where Merrick and Viki were drinking to celebrate success, Varden Two took his leave of the *Cherokee,* moving on his own mysterious mission.

Merrick stretched out an arm and slid it round Viki's waist, drawing the woman close and smiling down into her eyes. 'Well,' he whispered playfully, 'how do you like the idea of being queen of a reorganised world, my sweet?'

She pouted at him. 'Darling,' she replied, 'if being a queen means what I think it does, I'll love it!' She reached out for her glass of Scotch, raising it in a silent toast.

Merrick left her and strolled up and down the floor of the saloon, hands thrust in his pockets, a frown on his face. 'We've got to control the explosive nature of what we've started. In a few hours now, the entire world will be tearing itself to pieces in war. We've got to let it go on for just long enough to bring everyone down to their knees. Then we take the reins, Viki! My own interests can control almost the entire arms output of the world, and when we're ready — when the world is reduced — I can call a halt with a flick of my finger!'

'It sounds wonderful,' she whispered enthusiastically. 'But you're sure there's no danger of Blake and men like him putting a spoke in and wrecking our plans?'

Merrick laughed boisterously, slapping his thigh with a meaty hand. 'Viki!' he chided gently. 'You overestimate the risks. How can one man prevent a war? Or stop it once it starts?'

She considered thoughtfully for a moment, then nodded. 'You must be right,' she admitted. 'I was still thinking of that awful — whatever you'd call it — back in London. Darling, would the bomb we launched kill it?'

Merrick nodded firmly. 'Of course!' he said. 'Nothing could exist in the blast that thing will make. New York and London, Viki! Wrecked in a second! Not the whole of them, naturally, but enough to throw the nations into insanity and precipitate war. They'll be marching already!'

'Turn on the screen and take a look,' she said, rising to her feet and swaying towards him.

Merrick switched on a large video set, directing its unseen eye to various countries and cities. Everywhere were signs of hurried mobilisation, the rolling armies of tanks and machines, the assembled fleets of aircraft.

Merrick brought shattered London into

view. Fires still raged; rescue workers toiled like ants in the gloom of night and the glare of the arcs.

Viki's mouth quivered. 'Poor old London,' she whispered. 'I wish it didn't have to happen, honey.'

Merrick brushed it aside. 'Nonsense!' he exclaimed. 'In a few years we shall raise a greater city than London ever was!'

The hours passed till dawn was lightening the sky. Merrick and the woman watched fascinated as nations poured their forces into the field, the might of each separate bloc oiling slowly and relentlessly towards their enemies.

Then suddenly the video screen on which they watched began to fade.

Merrick cursed beneath his breath. 'Must be a failure!' he muttered. He pressed a bell, waiting till one of the crew appeared.

'Fix this damn thing!' he ordered curtly.

The seaman gulped. 'But, sir,' he stammered, 'something's wrong! Something ...'

The lights in the saloon and all over the *Cherokee* went out.

At the same time the skipper and the second-in-command looked at each other in bewilderment.

'What the hell?' roared the skipper. He seized the engine-room radio, banging it violently to and fro. Meanwhile the other officer was shouting into a microphone: 'What's gone wrong down below?' he bellowed.

A voice floated back at him, fading rapidly. Even the radio was failing. The skipper called a man from on deck. 'Tell those devils below to keep the engines running!' he yelled. In darkness another man showed up, coming from the engine room.

'Skipper!' he gasped. 'We've gone dead below. There ain't a light anywhere on the ship, but the dynamos are running perfectly. And the engines just stopped on their own! It — it ain't right! It's spooky, skipper!'

'I'll give you *spooky*!' roared the commander. He blundered out, running straight into Merrick. They crashed to the deck together.

Merrick was up first, cursing and swearing with a wild abandon that sprang as much from fear as from any other emotion. He seized the skipper by the collar and shook him violently till his teeth rattled.

'Damn you!' he screamed. 'What's the matter with this ship? What's the matter?'

The skipper tore himself free and landed a swift uppercut on Merrick's chin. Then he stood over the rapidly-sobered man.

'Now, you listen to me!' he snarled. 'You may own this ship, but I'm its captain. I don't know what's wrong with it; no one knows! You can take it that something's happened, and we're as good as derelict! Now get below and stay there!'

Merrick staggered back against the side of the deck house, his face a pale blur in the dawn. Suddenly he dragged out a gun from his pocket and shot the skipper in the chest. As the gun cracked, men came running from all directions.

Merrick waved them back from the fallen body of the man he had killed. 'Back to your posts!' he screamed. 'I won't have mutinous swine on the *Cherokee*!'

11

'Turn Away, Pilgrim'

'You!' gasped Varden grimly. 'I thought —'

'*— that I was blown to hell, eh? No, pal, I'm just like you in that respect. I rise from the fire like a phoenix!*' He did a brief caper, flapping his arms derisively.

Rhonna swung round at the abrupt sound of Varden's voice. She saw his staring eyes focused on nothing and guessed what had happened. Her fingers tightened on his arm convulsively as she sought to make him turn his head.

'It's here again?' she whispered. Luckily no one else in the big workshop had noticed Varden's sudden remark; they were all too engrossed in watching the glowing dome of milky luminance as it pulsed to some hidden force.

Varden turned his head slowly. 'Yes,' he breathed. 'Oh, Rhonna, what am I going to do? Is there no way out of this?'

Varden Two laughed harshly and insinuated himself between his other entity and the woman with auburn hair. He thrust his face into Varden's and grinned with all the evil of his soul.

'There's no way out!' he said. *'Nothing you can do will redeem us from our fate. We've walked with fools, and are paying for it now!'*

Varden thrust him aside, drawing Rhonna closer to him. 'Go away from me!' he whispered venomously. 'Get to hell out of here, you don't belong among decent people!'

Blake heard him say it and swung his head abruptly. 'What did you say, Varden?' he demanded.

Varden gritted his teeth, conscious that he was now the focus of a dozen pairs of eyes. Momentarily, the glowing dome was forgotten.

'I'm talking to myself,' he said sullenly. Blake understood or guessed what he meant. His eyes met those of his daughter and she nodded slightly.

'Take him to the screen room,' her father said. 'You'll be able to watch the results from there; the rest of us will join you presently.'

'*Rum old coot, isn't he? What's going on, Bob?*'

Varden ignored the question, turning and moving off with the woman. The others watched him curiously, then gave their attention to the dome again. Blake resumed his watch on the dials as if nothing had happened. After one look at his back, the second Varden followed Rhonna and her companion. They reached the screen room. Varden sank into a chair, covering his face to blot out the sight of the thing that was haunting him so remorselessly.

Rhonna put a hand on his shoulder. 'Try not to notice it, Bob,' she pleaded. 'I'm switching on the set.'

Varden raised his head, staring blankly at the screen. 'I'll try,' he said. 'It's right there beside you, though, and my eyes ... aren't as good as they were.'

The woman glanced apprehensively round, but her chin was firm and she was determined not to show any fear.

Varden Two was laughing quietly. '*As if I'd hurt her!*' he said sarcastically. '*Tired yet, Bob?*'

'No, I'm not tired! I'll never be tired

again!'

Rhonna glanced at him, but said nothing. The screen was coming to life now. Varden Two settled himself on the back of Varden's chair, one arm round Rhonna's neck and the other on his solid counterpart's shoulder. He was just as intent as they were on the scene shown by the video.

At first, it was similar to what Varden had already witnessed. Great fleets of war machines and aircraft moving relentlessly into battle in a dozen different zones. Then gradually a change was taking place. The mighty warships seemed to falter, slowing as they ploughed through the seas; the tanks rolled to a halt; men walked about in an agitated fashion searching, probing for faults; the vast squadrons of aircraft hesitated in flight, some dropped away towards the distant earth, out of control, others succeeded in gliding to safety, their engines dead.

'My God!' muttered Varden in amazement. 'What's happening?'

'Immobilisation of equipment,' she said with a smile. 'It's horribly drastic, of course, and will cost many lives, but there's nothing else to be done. We were too late to get

Merrick before he struck. This is the result.'

Varden Two gave a sigh. *'It's a shame to spoil a good war before it starts,'* he complained. *'Still, I take off my hat to Blake. Never seen a trick like it! Ask her how it's done, Bob.'*

Varden, too, was curious. He put the question to Rhonna, but she shook her head. 'Honestly,' she said, 'I couldn't explain it properly. You'll have to wait till Dad tells you.'

Varden grunted, rubbing a hand over his face as his vision dimmed again. The woman shot him an anxious glance. Varden said, 'Don't take any notice of what I say next, Rhonna. I'm going to ask my — my shadow something.'

She nodded. Her hands were busy with the tuning controls of the video.

Varden said, 'Listen, is your eyesight all right?'

'Never been better, brother! You suffering? Maybe it's because you've led such a wicked life! I'll let you know if I can't see properly.'

Varden was quiet. They differed in that respect anyway, he thought bitterly. He was going blind again. He knew as surely as he knew anything, and the knowledge did little to cheer him in his already unhappy state of mind.

Blake and several of his assistants came in then. Varden Two contented himself with passing remarks, mostly obscene, about their characteristics. Varden did not pass them on. Most of the assistants, talking quietly and grimly among themselves, took their places at other videos, tuning the sets over a wide area of the world's surface.

Blake joined Varden and Rhonna. 'Well?' he said slowly. 'How is it now?'

Varden smiled dispiritedly. 'What have you achieved?' he inquired. 'I'm amazed by what seems to be going on, but I don't quite follow. How does this immobilisation stop war? If men lose their aircraft, tanks or ships, they use their feet and fight with their hands.'

Blake gave a grim smile. 'You haven't seen it all, my friend,' he said. 'Take a close look at the screens. What do they tell you?'

Varden glanced round hurriedly, noting that his other self was on the opposite side of the room, leaning over the shoulder of a scientist with blond hair and spectacles, a tired young man. Then he gave his attention to the screen Rhonna was working.

As she moved the controls, he saw a large powerhouse on the outskirts of a city. There was snow on the hills in the background, and a partly-frozen river wound its course through wooded country. Crowds of people, men and women, stood about in front of the powerhouse, helpless expressions on their blank, white faces.

'The machinery is dead,' murmured Blake. 'In that city, Bob, there is no light, no heat from electrical sources or the local atomic pile, no communications or video. Everything of a mechanical nature in which electricity plays any part whatsoever is useless. Now do you begin to understand how we stopped the war?'

'But how?' he demanded. 'I see that everything's halted, but how? And what's to prevent them fighting on in a more old-fashioned manner?'

Blake permitted himself a smile. 'They'll have to fight with short-range rifles and pistols,' he said. 'Don't forget that the majority of modern weapons are fired electronically, as well as sighted and ranged by the same medium. No, Varden, the war is virtually over before it began; unless we give the nations time to readjust themselves and get in touch with one another, when they may start up again on the lines I mentioned.'

'It'll take time, of course,' Varden mused. He was still dazed by what he had seen; and stunned, too, by the magnitude of the resultant chaos.

'But look,' he said suddenly. 'What about the starvation and disease arising out of this? The whole world depends for its food and medicine on transport and electrical equipment. Now that you've worked some magic to destroy that source of power, people will die in their millions!' He glared at the scientist savagely for an instant. 'My God, you've committed a worse sin than Merrick ever did in starting this business!'

Blake only shook his head, not condemning Varden for what he said. 'Soon,' he said, slowly, 'my men will go out to right the position. They will make broadcasts from the sky above every city of importance, explaining, calling for a sensible approach to permanent peace.'

Varden hesitated. 'And if it fails?'

Blake shrugged. 'In that case, we shall have to use our power as a weapon instead of a preventive.'

'You mean …?'

'Yes, what the devil does he mean, Bob?'

Blake said, 'We can turn this disruptive force on or off at will, you realise. Only if the peoples of the world agree to put aside their arms, at least for the time being, will we turn it off for sufficiently long to enable countries to restore order and feed themselves.'

'If they refuse to listen to reason,' Varden mused, 'it will mean complete chaos and widespread death.'

'Dad wouldn't leave it on for long enough,' put in Rhonna. 'Not even if the nations were obstinate. Controlled from here, it could be used at any time as a deterrent, but he'll try to make them *think* they're completely in is power — until they pull themselves together and reach an agreement.'

'I must say the plan has its points, Bob. We're in the wrong business, you and I! Think of what a man could do with this thing if he handled it sensibly!' The entity

was carried away by the vistas of corruption opened up before him.

Varden lost his temper and went for him, but the unseen being was in playful mood, though the brief encounter seriously upset everyone else in the screen room. Finally Rhonna grabbed hold of Varden and hung on to him tightly.

'Stop it!' she cried. 'Stop it, both of you!'

Varden Two breathed hard for a moment, then bowed cynically. *'The lady's right,'* he said. *'We ought to behave like gentlemen, brother! Forgive me, please!'*

Varden allowed himself to be pushed into a chair before one of the videos. Blake made some hurried explanations to the group of astounded assistants. None of them showed the surprise Varden would have expected; but then, he reflected, they, like Blake, were scientists. Perhaps such a phenomenon as a double entity was not so strange to their minds as it was to his own.

Rhonna was studying the screen again, ignoring the aftermath of what had happened. Everywhere there were signs of panic as people began to realise the position they were in. For the first time in their lives, they understood how much they depended on electricity and its derivatives for their daily existence.

Blake said: 'You probably still wonder how this is done, Bob. Can you comprehend an impulse sufficiently powerful to break down the insulating properties of materials employed in electrical equipment? By that, I mean an impulse which itself creates a field of energy surrounding any appliance of a current-carrying nature. Wires, condensers, and so on. The resulting field of energy tends to break down the current-resisting power of all affected gear.' He peered at Varden intently, seeking to get his message across. 'The effect, as you can imagine, is one of short-circuiting vital parts of almost all modern machines from a car to a ship, or even an electronically-fired weapon.'

Varden frowned deeply, glancing first at Rhonna, then at the face of his other entity. Varden Two whistled softly.

'Lord,' he grunted, *'what a scheme! You've got to admit the old boy knows his stuff! But wait a minute ... Isn't there a flaw in his present plan, Bob?'*

'I don't see it,' said Varden defensively.

'No, Blake, I don't mean I don't understand. I — I'm talking to *this*.' He pointed
vaguely. 'It says there's a flaw.'

*'Of course there is! How the dickens is
he going to fly around with his precious ultimatum if the impulse field is in operation?
Ask him to get over that one!'*

'A flaw?' murmured Blake, with a worried frown. 'I thought we'd made provision
for all the snags.'

Varden said, 'If the impulse is general,
what about your plans to fly over cities? And
anyway … ' His voice trailed off as another
thought crossed his mind.

Blake smiled. 'I should have told you,' he
apologised. 'It's a simple matter to screen
our own equipment from the force field.'
He chuckled. 'How did you imagine it was
possible to sit here and watch these videos
if not?'

Varden grinned. 'The same thought just
came to me,' he said. 'Then you have planes
ready standing by, unaffected by this?'

'Naturally.' He glanced at his watch. 'In
about thirty minutes, when the full implica-
tion of what has happened begins to dawn on
the nations of the world, my men will leave.'

'It might work out,' said Varden thoughtfully. 'I wish I could be as sure as you are, though.'

'Don't worry,' put in Rhonna. 'We've got faith enough in Dad to see it through.'

Varden Two simpered in a corner where he was standing. Then: *'I'd love to see old Merrick's face right now!'* he said. *'He was none too happy about life when I paid him a visit just after the launching of the paired projectiles. Now he must be tearing out his hair — what he's got left of it.'*

Varden blinked. 'You know whereabouts he is?' he demanded.

The other man snorted. *'Of course I do, pal! I know a lot of things. I could give you the exact position of the yacht* Cherokee *if it hasn't drifted far since the 'fluence came on. In fact, I've a damn good mind to let you have it and see what you make of it!'*

Varden sat very still, his eyes closed because pain shot through them in blinding spasms. 'Give it to me if you feel like that,' he said flatly.

Varden Two considered, then shrugged. *'You're going blind again, Bob,'* he reminded him. *'You can't even see the redhead clearly, and you know it. Maybe I will give you Merrick's position so you'll know you've failed.'* He grinned. *'Pardon my distorted sense of humour, brother!'*

Varden got his eyes working again, opened them and peered round. Everyone in the room was watching him.

'Give me that position,' he said grimly.

As if knowing exactly what was going on, Rhonna pushed a pad and pencil in front of him.

Varden Two put his head on one side, watching Varden with cruel, calculating eyes. *'34 degrees 21 north, 30 degrees 15 east,'* he said. *'I'm leaving you now, Bob, but have the old man send one of his stooges to the* Cherokee. *I'll just love to hear what Merrick has to say when he gets the ultimatum! 'Bye.'*

Varden glanced round, seeing only the puzzled, curious faces of his companions.

'Those figures, Bob ... What do they represent?' asked Blake.

'The spot where Merrick is,' he replied. 'My unholy twin suggested you send one of your planes to tell him what's happened.'

Blake hesitated. 'Not worth it,' he said.

'He'll be dealt with later on when the world sees reason: in the meantime, we've too many other things to do.'

Varden sat staring at the figures he had jotted down. His eyes were dimming over more frequently now. He reached out a hand and felt for Rhonna at his side. She seemed to read his need, for she guided him out of the screen room and up the steps to the farm house above.

'Sit down,' she said, gently. 'Is it very bad, Bob?'

He began to focus again, to see through the thick curtain of dullness that clouded his vision. 'Better now, thanks,' he muttered. 'Rhonna, the other thing's gone again. It's wonderful what a difference it makes when it's not around.' He tried to smile. 'I feel almost free.'

'You will be free,' she whispered. 'Things'll be all right before long, you'll see.'

He looked at her closely. It was all there in her green-coloured eyes, and he knew it. He stood up abruptly. There were some things he couldn't stand. 'Please don't,' he said. 'It — it isn't any use, my dear. I've got to sort this out for myself, without your help or anyone else's.'

She watched him for a moment, then came up behind him, her hand going to his shoulder in mute appeal. 'Bob,' she said, very quietly. 'Do you think I don't understand how you feel? Do you think I don't know what's going on in your mind? Why not admit it? We belong to each other, you and I.'

He turned and met her gaze. All the cravings inside him were crystallised in this one woman. He longed to close his mind to the bitterness and defeat that haunted him, seeking release in the warmth and comfort she offered so graciously. Yet he knew it was impossible. There could be no such future, nor even the dreams that centred round it.

'Don't!' he said harshly. He thrust her aside, walking blindly to the outer door, hurrying.

Rhonna fell back, her mouth trembling. 'Bob,' she breathed. 'Bob, don't run away like that.'

But Varden didn't hear what she said. Even had he done so, he would not have stopped. He dare not turn his head for fear of breaking his self-control, dare not look back at what he wanted so badly. Outside, by the clustered buildings of the farm, the small, fast jet helicopters were being wheeled out and started. There was still something Varden had to do. After that ... It didn't matter a lot; nothing would matter anymore. He walked fast, heading for the nearest of the aircraft.

12

And Darkness Came

34, 21 north; 30, 15 east ... The numerals were running through and through his head as he approached the plane. There was still something he had to do, unfinished business. His eyes blurred over as one of Blake's assistants came and spoke to the mechanic at the plane. Varden halted, rubbing his forehead. He mustn't waste time, he thought desperately. There was so little time. He stood quite still, swaying his head from side to side, fighting to see through the curtain of darkness that threatened him.

The aircraft engines were running all round him now. The softly muted hum of the turbines sang a danger signal in his ears. He couldn't fail now, not whatever happened.

'Thanks, Jim,' the assistant was saying. 'She's all right for fuel, eh? Long trip to make.'

Varden could not see the man called Jim. He could not see the assistant. All round him was thickening darkness, yet the sun was bright and warm on his shoulders.

'You going to Moscow, sir?' the mechanic inquired. 'Hope you make 'em see sense.'

'They will,' came the answer, grim but confident. 'They will have little choice. The same goes for all other countries.'

Varden began to see again. The man who was bound for Moscow was stepping into the waiting plane. Varden lurched forward, seeing only his objective. From somewhere behind him he heard Rhonna's voice, calling anxiously. She was calling him, guessing his intentions perhaps. The young man was half in the plane now. He turned and jumped down at the sound of Rhonna's cry.

'What's the matter?' he called, puzzled.

Varden came round the tail of the plane. He hit the mechanic between the eyes as the man tried to intercept him. The assistant swung round to face him. Varden lashed out with all the savage fury of a desperate man. Then he was inside the aircraft as Rhonna came running towards it.

'Bob, don't do it!' she begged. Her hands

were stretched out pleadingly. Varden turned his head as he banged the engines open. He grinned at her, raising his hand in salute as the two men struggled to their feet. Others were racing towards the plane now, their numbers swelling as they came. They stopped as the helicopter rose from the ground. Varden watched them growing smaller, watched the horizon increase in its broad expanse. He saw Blake below, with Rhonna staring up at the sky. For one wild instant he thought he saw tears on her cheeks, glistening in the sunshine. Then he turned away, too full of emotion to fight the longing that urged him to land again.

34, 21 north, 30, 15 east ... Working as much by instinct as by knowledge of the machine, he set course and watched the rolling countryside unfold below. Looking back, he could see no sign of pursuit — nor did he expect it. Rhonna knew well enough where he was bound for; she'd guessed it. Blake would make no attempt to stop him now. Flying south at first, he saw lines of stationary vehicles on every road he crossed. In fields and on aerodromes, hundreds of battle planes stood idle, with knots of men moving aimlessly this way and that, defeated by the very engines they relied on. And when Varden turned the plane out across the sea, there were drifting, stationary fleets beyond the harbours. Going low over one great battleship, he saw uniformed men waving frantically to him. A seaman started semaphoring with flags. He remembered that not even an Aldis signal lamp would work now. He was almost sorry for these men who did not understand and could get no word from their fellows below the horizon.

Miles away, be saw the floating fuselages of several large aircraft, half-submerged. Poor devils, he thought. He did not fly near them; there was nothing he could do for the crews. They had come down bewildered, and would die bewildered, without hope of succour.

★ ★ ★

Merrick stood squarely on the *Cherokee*'s bridge, his eyes hot with anger. The entire crew was ranged in a group on deck, and they stared at Merrick balefully, glancing from him to the body of their skipper.

Merrick held a gun in his hand, covering them with it, his gaze raking them in mingled fear and fury.

'I want this ship running again in an hour!' he shouted. 'If any man turns mutinous I'll shoot him myself. You saw what happened before.'

The chief engineer stepped forward. His jaw was working and he clenched his fists as he looked up at the owner.

'I've already made my report,' he said, curtly. 'Nothing on board with the remotest connection to electrical power works. All gear is in perfect order, but it doesn't work any more.'

Merrick's jowls quivered. 'I don't care what you say!' he bellowed. 'I want this ship moving if you have to paddle it along!'

The men muttered among themselves. One shouldered forward, but Merrick's instant reaction made him change his mind. Even the chief engineer gave a shrug and turned away. 'If you ask me,' he said to another, 'something damn funny's gone wrong with the whole blinking set-up. Radio dead, video dead. Why, even my flashlamp doesn't work! There's a jinx on us, mate!'

They growled and grumbled, the second-in-command detailing two men to carry the skipper's body to his cabin, It was a gloomy little procession. Merrick stood on deck and watched.

Viki ventured from the saloon to join Merrick. She was frightened and made no pretence at hiding the fact. But Merrick offered her very little comfort; he had enough worries on his mind as it was. For the first time he began to realise that the yacht was completely isolated, a drifting hulk as it rolled on the broad Atlantic.

'Could — could this be anything to do with Blake?' the woman asked nervously.

He swung on her. 'Blake!' he shouted. 'Act your age! How could one man do this?' He paused. 'No, it's just our luck, that's all. These swine who call themselves sailors will put it right if I have to shoot 'em one by one till they do! Now get below and stay there!'

Sudden hate blazed in her eyes as she saw the vicious transformation of Merrick into what he really was. In a strained tone, she said, 'You devil ...You utter devil!' She sprang at him, clawing wildly.

Merrick hit her with the barrel of his gun, in the mouth. She swayed, stumbled, and fell heavily to the deck. Blood formed a little pool near her head. She twitched, and after a while lay still. Her breathing was hard.

The big man, suddenly panic-stricken, dropped to his knees beside her, gabbling phrases and begging her to listen. She did not answer; he stared aghast at what he had done, then covered his face with his hands. Then something began to happen that chilled his blood. The pool of blood by Viki's head suddenly had a stick thrust in it from nowhere: gruesome words began to appear on the deck floor as the stick scrawled on it.

Merrick backed away in fear, his eyes wide, all colour drained from his face, rigid in the grip of terror.

'Words!' he gasped. 'Oh, no — not that ... Not that!'

And the unseen Varden sniggered as he scrawled the stick along, forming the words in scarlet: *You've done it wrong, Merrick. Blake's beaten you. You're finished. So's Viki, by the look of it. Too rough in your passion, brother — too rough.'*

Varden sat back on his heels, cynically amused by Merrick's terror. He wished he could drive this man mad — just to watch *that* would amuse him. There was no other reason. Merrick's eyes were glassy now. Varden scratched his chin reflectively, then leant over, chuckling, and touched the man on the face with the stick. Merrick recoiled as if he had been smitten with the very rod of the Devil himself. The big man lashed out wildly at his unseen antagonist, vainly, then screamed.

Viki had almost stopped bleeding.

Merrick staggered to the ship's rail, leaned over it drunkenly, trying to keep his stomach still. And Varden Two sat by Viki's still form, watching it, taking vindictive pleasure in the mental havoc he'd wrought.

The second officer came up from below and stared in amazement. His eyes went from Viki to Merrick, then back again. He coughed. 'Excuse me, sir,' he said. 'There's a plane coming up from the north-east ...'

Merrick dragged himself erect; swaying, ashen. A jet helicopter was streaking in towards them, the whine of its engines mounting each second.

Varden One checked and circled the ship, verifying that it was his target. Then he landed on the aft deck, was surrounded at once by the crew as they yelled questions at him in their greed for news. Merrick, unsteady, forced a path through them as Varden clambered out of the plane. Close on Merrick's heels came Varden Two, unholy glee lighting his eyes.

Varden One stood facing Merrick, and a sudden hush fell. The crew froze into immobility where they stood.

'You!' croaked Merrick hoarsely.

Varden nodded grimly, moving towards him. He had to get close because there was a mist across his eyes again, a thicker fog of blurring than before, closing in round him, localising his vision. He cursed it, knowing that only blindness could beat him.

'You should see what he's done to little Viki,' said the other Varden. *'This is good, brother; keep on coming!'*

And Varden kept coming. Merrick fell back before his slow, relentless advance. The hand in which he gripped the gun was shaking. He was standing now against the wheel-house where Viki lay slumped, her blood-soaked torso ugly in dumb repose.

'What do you want?' stammered Merrick wildly. 'Take him away,' he added in a scream to the men. They looked on with stolid curiosity, not moving to obey. 'Take him away!'

'Take it easy with the gent, Bob.'

'You keep out of this!' snarled Varden. He glanced round, seeking a weapon, finding none. Merrick's eyes were bulging in their sockets. Varden could barely see him now: a great black circle was tightening round the face of his enemy, slowly blotting it out.

He drew closer and closer, moving with a panther-like step. Merrick trod sideways, putting his foot in the pool of blood from Viki, smearing the message scrawled on the deck. His foot slipped as he trod. Varden did not see the blood or the body — he could only just see Merrick now. And Merrick turned to run, too terrified even to use his gun.

Varden leapt on him just as he turned. His other entity gave a howl of satisfaction, capering about like a madman. The watching crew sucked their breath in sharply as

Varden's fingers closed on Merrick's arm and whirled him round. As if instilled with the strength of a giant, Varden gripped him and held him. Then he turned to face the crew.

'Because of this man, the world was threatened by war,' he said quietly. 'Thousands died in London and New York when he launched his bombs. I was there, and I know! And because I was there, I've come after him. I've come to kill him.'

He tried to shake the mist from his eyes but it refused to go. Darkness was closing in on him. A deeper darkness than ever. He could no longer see the faces of the men, the sun or the sea.

'You're going to die, Merrick,' he continued. 'And you're going to know before you die that you've failed.'

Merrick seemed to pull himself together. As Varden felt for and found his throat he brought his gun up and pressed it against the body of his enemy. Varden's fingers were tightening steel on his windpipe. He pressed the trigger so that Varden jerked to the blasting concussion of the shots. He felt the bullets tearing at his flesh, going through him like red-hot wires. Merrick emptied the magazine, splitting Varden's stomach across, killing him a dozen times over. And Varden went on choking the life from his body, killing him by slow degrees till he sagged to the deck, a lifeless, unbreathing corpse.

Varden straightened up and turned very slowly. He felt no pain, felt nothing but the closing in of the darkness on his eyes. It didn't lift this time.

'Lord!' gasped one of the men. 'Look! His guts are hanging out! Why ain't he dead?' There was superstitious terror in his cry.

Varden grinned. 'I can't die,' he muttered. 'Nothing can kill me. Nothing, you understand?'

He walked blindly towards the sound of the babbling voices that rose at his words. Men were fighting to get out of his way as he advanced. One fetched a light machine gun from the wheel-house, panic rising in his heart as he trained it on Varden. Varden kept walking, swaying a little. At his side walked the other Varden. They passed close to Viki. She opened her eyes and saw him, the visible one. From her shattered mouth came a frightful scream as she struggled up. Then the clatter of the gun began its mad tattoo. Bullets tore into Varden's body, ripping the flesh from his frame, tearing at his skull and opening his throat. He walked blindly on, towards the stern of the *Cherokee*.

The men watched in horror. Behind the machine gun, the man who worked it went raving mad. He went on firing till the ammunition ran out. Varden's body took and absorbed the repeated impact of the bullets, but he never stopped walking till he and the second Varden reached the stern rail. Then, as if bound together by invisible cords, they paused, hesitated, and finally felt their way over the rail. The final burst of gunfire sheared the top off Varden's skull, sending fragments of hair and bloody tissue in a splatter to the water below. Varden turned and lifted his hand in salute to the men he could no longer see.

'They don't like us,' muttered his companion. *'We aren't wanted any more.'*

Varden made no answer. His lower jaw had been cut away completely by the hail of bullets. From his throat there came a dreadful gurgling grunt. The blindness of death enveloped him.

Viki gave a scream that echoed to the very skies. As if trying to reach the stern, she staggered forward. There was one more cartridge in the gunbelt. She took it in the spine, flopping over the rail as Varden and his unseen companion dropped from sight. And the stillness of death was round them ...

★   ★   ★

Varden felt delicate fingers moving against his skin. 'You mustn't expect too much at first,' someone told him quietly. Light seeped in through his closed eyelids, forcing him to open them. There was pain and dimness, the sickness and the smells and the fear of blindness all round him.

Pale green walls seen dimly; the dizzying face of someone bending over him; the crisp feel of linen and the even warmth of shadowed sunshine.

Someone said, 'A success, I think. That grafting did the trick, but it was touch and go for a time.'

Varden said, 'I am alone, aren't I?'

'Yes, of course you are, old man. Did you

think …?'

His lips moved cautiously. 'It's all right,' he said. 'No one else in the bed … I — I thought there was at first.'

Two doctors and a nurse with a stiffly starched uniform exchanged glances. One of the doctors shrugged. 'No,' he said. 'You're alone in bed, Varden.'

'Thank God for that! There was someone, but he's gone'

'Yes, of course. You take it easy for a while now.'

'Thanks.' He remembered the cold water engulfing him: the indeterminate period during which he sank and sank and finally floated. There was darkness and light and darkness and noise. He didn't remember anything more …

Time passed monotonously. The room was dim, with someone sitting in a far corner: he couldn't see who it was, probably a nurse. She came and straightened his pillows, made the light even dimmer. He slept. He didn't think about anything; there was nothing to think about now; he didn't want to think.

Then someone said: 'You'll remember,

won't you, that he mustn't be disturbed too much at this stage?'

Another voice replied: 'Of course, and thank you for letting me see him.'

'Hello,' someone said. 'Hello, Bob. I thought you'd like someone to talk to.'

He turned his head a little, pushing aside the swimming feeling inside it, grasping at something solid and understandable.

'Who's that?' he asked quietly. 'It isn't Viki, and it can't be Merrick because you're not a man. No one else would visit me. I'm not blind now, you know. I can see. They did an operation ... Something to do with grafting.'

'No,' said the voice. 'It isn't Viki. Or Merrick. It's Rhonna. I — I just thought ... '

'Rhonna?' he echoed. 'But you didn't like me!' He could see her now, see the sleek auburn hair, the green-coloured eyes, the little flecks of brown in their depths. 'I don't deserve this,' he muttered.

'Would you rather have Viki to see you?'

He considered that before answering. Then: 'Not really,' he admitted. He peered at her in the dimness of the room.

'Rhonna,' he said. 'Do you happen to

have a mirror?'

'Afraid of what you look like?' She opened her handbag. 'I suppose I shouldn't do this really, but you'll think all kinds of horrible things if I don't.'

She held out a square of glass. His face was thin and gaunt, with one long burn scar down the line of his jaw. He handed the mirror back. 'Better than I expected,' he murmured.

'You were lucky,' she said. 'Lucky in more ways than one.'

'What do you mean by that?'

'Something happened in New York,' she said. 'I'm glad you wouldn't rather have Viki here than me.'

Varden stiffened. 'I meant that, Rhonna.'

'She's dead, anyway. She and Merrick too.'

Varden lay quiet for a moment. Then: 'How?'

'The F.B.I. were after them for subversive activities likely to start a war,' she replied. 'Merrick was fool enough to put up a fight. They were both shot dead in the battle.' She broke off. 'That was the day after you crashed in the sea, Bob.'

'Then there isn't any war, after all? I'm glad now. And your father ... ?'

She smiled. 'He's still working on preventive measures.'

A queer expression crossed his face. 'At the farm in Scotland?' he queried.

She frowned. 'How did you know? It's supposed to be a secret. Bob, what do you know about it?'

'A lot of things I don't want to think about. Forget it. But tell me this: What's the date?'

'August the twenty-fourth,' she replied, bewildered.

'And the year?'

'2017, of course!'

Varden sighed gratefully and closed his eyes. 'That's fine,' he whispered. His hand crept out and closed on her fingers. A nurse and a little fat doctor with rimless glasses came in.

Varden said, 'Hello, doc. You did a good job. How?'

The rimless glasses flashed. 'A graft of the optic nerve, my boy. Delicate, but entirely successful. Luckily for you there was healthy material on hand.' He chuckled.

'Some hours after they brought you in, another patient died. We used what we needed from him.'

Varden nodded slowly. 'Who was he, doc?'

'We don't reveal names,' came the answer. 'He was one of these professional clairvoyant people. An interesting case all round.'

'Very,' said Varden thoughtfully. 'When do I get out of here, doc? I might want to fix up a wedding.'

The doctor grinned. 'You relax for a time,' he said. 'She'll be waiting!'

We do hope that you have enjoyed reading this large print book.

Did you know that all of our titles are available for purchase?

We publish a wide range of high quality large print books including:
Romances, Mysteries, Classics
General Fiction
Non Fiction and Westerns

Special interest titles available in large print are:
The Little Oxford Dictionary
Music Book, Song Book
Hymn Book, Service Book

Also available from us courtesy of Oxford University Press:
Young Readers' Dictionary
(large print edition)
Young Readers' Thesaurus
(large print edition)

For further information or a free brochure, please contact us at:
Ulverscroft Large Print Books Ltd.,
The Green, Bradgate Road, Anstey,
Leicester, LE7 7FU, England.
Tel: (00 44) **0116 236 4325**
Fax: (00 44) **0116 234 0205**

PHANTOM HOLLOW

Gerald Verner

When Tony Frost and his colleague Jack Denton arrive for a holiday at Monk's Lodge, an ancient cottage deep in the Somerset countryside, they are immediately warned off by the local villagers and a message scrawled in crimson across a windowpane: 'THERE IS DANGER. GO WHILE YOU CAN!' Tony invites his friend, the famous dramatist and criminologist Trevor Lowe, to come and help — but the investigation takes a sinister turn when the dead body of a missing estate agent is found behind a locked door in the cottage . . .

THE DEVIL IN HER

Norman Firth

The Devil in Her sees Doctor Alan Carter returning to England to stay with an old friend, Colonel Merton, after seven arduous years abroad — only to receive a terrible shock. He first encounters frightened locals who tell him tales of a ghostly woman in filmy white roaming the moors and slaughtering animals. Dismissing their warnings, he proceeds to Merton Lodge — and into a maze of mystery and death. While in *She Vamped a Strangler*, private detective Rodney Granger investigates a case of robbery and murder in the upper echelons of society.

FURY DRIVES BY NIGHT

Denis Hughes

Captain Guy Conway of the British Secret Intelligence sets out to investigate Fortune Cay, a three-hundred-year-old cottage on the Yorkshire coast. The current owner is being terrorised by his new neighbour, who Guy fears could be his arch-nemesis, an international mercenary and war criminal whom he thought he had killed towards the end of the Second World War. En route to the cottage, Conway rescues an unconscious woman from her crashed car — only to find that their lives are inextricably linked as they fight to cheat death . . .

JESSICA'S DEATH

Tony Gleeson

Detectives Jilly Garvey and Dan Lee are no strangers to violent death. Nevertheless, the brutal killing of an affluent woman, whose body is found in a decaying urban neighborhood miles from her home, impacts them deeply. Their investigative abilities are stretched to the limit as clues don't add up and none of the possible suspects seem quite right. As they dig deeper into the background of the victim, a portrait emerges of a profoundly troubled woman. Will they find the answers they need to bring a vicious killer to justice?

41. From mental purity (arises) purity of *Sattva*, cheerful-mindedness, one-pointedness, control of the senses and fitness for the vision of the Self.

The above *Sūtra* gives the results of inner or mental purity. While the other three results which follow from mental purity are easily understandable, some explanation is necessary with regard to *Sattva-Śuddhi*. It has already been shown that the Hindu conception of the manifested world with all its multifarious phenomena is based on the three underlying *Guṇas*—*Sattva*, *Rajas* and *Tamas*. It has also been pointed out that *Sattva*, the *Guṇa* corresponding to equilibrium alone can enable the mind to reflect consciousness. In fact, it is clear from the many *Sūtras* bearing on the subject that the aim of the *Yogi*, as far as his vehicles are concerned, is to eliminate *Rajas* and *Tamas* and make *Sattva* as predominant as possible in order that his *Citta* may mirror the *Puruṣa* to the maximum degree. So that, from the highest point of view purification is the fundamental problem involved in Self-realization and this purification consists essentially in the gradual elimination of the *Rājasic* and *Tāmasic* elements from *Citta* working at different levels. Of course, this elimination is only comparative. To reduce *Rajas* and *Tamas* to zero would be to reduce the *Guṇas* to a state of perfect equilibrium and to take consciousness completely out of manifestation as indicated in IV-34. *Sattva-Śuddhi* is, therefore, the interpretation of purification in terms of the *Guṇas* as both change *pari passu*.

It will also be seen that *Sattva-Śuddhi* is the fundamental change involved in inner purification and the other three results which are brought about are the natural consequences of this change. For, all those conditions mentioned in I-31 which are the accompaniments of *Vikṣepa* are the result of the predominance of *Rājasic* and *Tāmasic* elements in our nature. A disturbed and disharmonized mind is certainly not fit for the vision of the Self.

४२. संतोषादनुत्तमः सुखलाभः ।

Saṃtoṣād anuttamaḥ sukha-lābhaḥ.

संतोषात् from contentment अनुत्तम: unexcelled; unsurpassed
सुख (of) happiness लाभ: gain.

42.　Superlative happiness from contentment.

The result of developing perfect contentment is superlative
happiness.　This is quite natural.　The chief cause of our constant
unhappiness is the perpetual disturbance of the mind caused by
all kinds of desires.　When a particular desire is satisfied there is
a temporary cessation of this unhappiness which by comparison
we feel as happiness but the other latent desires soon assert themselves and we lapse again into the normal condition of unhappiness.　We sometimes feel that we are quite desireless.　This feeling
is illusory.　The absence of desire in the conscious mind at
any time does not necessarily mean that we have become desireless.　There may be innumerable desires, and some of them very
strong, hidden within our sub-conscious mind.　These in their
totality produce a general feeling of discontentment even when
there is no strong desire present in the conscious mind.　Real and
perfect contentment follows the elimination of our personal desires
which are the source of unhappiness.

It may be objected that the absence of unhappiness does not
necessarily mean the presence of happiness which is a positive
state of the mind.　There is a definite reason why superlative
happiness abides in a perfectly calm and contented mind.　A
calm mind is able to reflect within itself the bliss which is inherent
in our real Divine nature.　The constant surging of desires pre-
vents this bliss from manifesting itself in the mind.　It is only
when these desires are eliminated and the mind becomes perfectly
calm that we know what true happiness is.　This subtle and constant joy which is called *Sukha* and which comes from within is
independent of external circumstances and is really a reflection of
Ananda, one of the three fundamental aspects of the Self.

४३.　कायेन्द्रियसिद्धिरशुद्धिक्षयात् तपसः ।

Kāyendriya-siddhir aśuddhi-kṣayāt tapasaḥ.

काय the body इन्द्रिय sense-organs सिद्धि: occult powers; perfection अशुद्धि impurity क्षयात् on (gradual) destruction तपस: from
austerities.

43. Perfection of the sense-organs and body after
destruction of impurity by austerities.

The word *Siddhi* is used in two senses. It means both occult
power and perfection. Here, obviously, the word has been used
chiefly in the latter sense. The development of *Siddhis* connected
with the body takes place on *Bhūta-Jaya* or mastery of *Bhūtas* as
shown in III-46. Since *Bhūta-Jaya* also leads to the perfection of
the body—*Kāya-Sampat*—as defined in III-47, the perfection of the
body implied in II-43 is of a different and lower kind than that
in III-47. The perfection meant here is obviously functional,
i.e. it enables the *Yogi* to use the body for the purposes of *Yoga*
without any kind of resistance or hindrance from it.

Since the essential purpose of *Tapas* is to purify the body and
bring it under the control of the will as explained in II-32 it will
be easily seen why it should culminate in the functional perfection of the body. It is the presence of impurity in the body
and lack of control which stands in the way of its being used as
a perfect instrument of consciousness. The function of the sense-
organs also becomes perfect because this function is really
dependent upon the currents of *Prāṇa* which are brought under
the control of the *Yogi* by practices like those of *Prāṇāyāma*.
Prāṇāyāma is considered to be *Tapas par excellence*. As the practice
of austerities does sometimes lead to the development of some of
the lower *Siddhis* in the case of people who are especially sensitive
the word *Siddhi* may be considered to be used in both the senses
given above.

The significance of the phrase *Aśuddhi-kṣayāt* should be kept in
mind. It shows conclusively that the removal of impurity is the
main purpose of performing *Tapas* and also that it is only when the
body has been completely purified that it can function perfectly
as an instrument of consciousness.

४४. स्वाध्यायादिष्टदेवतासंप्रयोग: ।

Svādhyāyād iṣṭa-devatā-samprayogaḥ.

स्वाध्यायात् from self-study (the study which leads to knowledge of the Self) इष्टदेवता (with) the desired deity संप्रयोग: union
or communion; coming into touch.

44.   By (or from) self-study union with the desired
deity.

Svādhyāya attains its acme in communion with the *Iṣṭa-Devatā*
because that is its ultimate purpose. As has been shown in II-32
although *Svādhyāya* begins with the study of problems relating to
spiritual life its main purpose is to open up a channel between the
Sādhaka and the object of his search. The nature of this communion will differ according to the temperament and capacity of
the *Sādhaka* and the nature of the *Iṣṭa-Devatā*. The essential
element in such a communion is the free flow of knowledge, power
and guidance from the higher to the lower consciousness.

४५.   समाधिसिद्धिरीश्वरप्रणिधानात् ।

Samādhi-siddhir Īśvara-praṇidhānāt.

समाधि trance सिद्धि: success; accomplishment; perfection ईश्वर
(to) God प्रणिधानात् from self-surrender; from resignation.

45.   Accomplishment of *Samādhi* from resignation
to God.

The fact that *Īśvara-Praṇidhāna* can lead ultimately to *Samādhi*
is a startling revelation. This fact has already been referred to in
I-23 where Patañjali not only points out the possibility of attaining
Samādhi through *Īśvara-Praṇidhāna* but also in subsequent *Sūtras*